OUTSIDE
THE LINE

OUTSIDE
THE LINE

Christian Petersen

A Castle Street Mystery

DUNDURN PRESS
TORONTO

Editor: Michael Carroll   Design: Courtney Horner
                 Printer: Webcom

Library and Archives Canada Cataloguing in Publication
Petersen, Christian
        Outside the line / by Christian Petersen.
(A Castle Street mystery)
ISBN 978-1-55002-859-1
        I. Title. II. Series: Castle Street mystery
PS8581.E83O98 2009   C813'.54   C2008-906219-1

1   2   3   4   5   13   12   11   10   09

Conseil des Arts du Canada   Canada Council for the Arts   ONTARIO ARTS COUNCIL CONSEIL DES ARTS DE L'ONTARIO

We acknowledge the support of **The Canada Council for the Arts** and the **Ontario Arts Council** for our publishing program. We also acknowledge the financial support of the **Government of Canada** through the **Book Publishing Industry Development Program** and **The Association for the Export of Canadian Books**, and the **Government of Ontario** through the **Ontario Book Publishers Tax Credit program**, and the **Ontario Media Development Corporation**.

Printed and bound in Canada
www.dundurn.com

Dundurn Press
3 Church Street, Suite 500
Toronto, Ontario, Canada
M5E 1M2

Gazelle Book Services Limited
White Cross Mills
High Town, Lancaster, England
LA1 4XS

Dundurn Press
2250 Military Road
Tonawanda, NY
U.S.A. 14150

To Ann

*For Peter
in memory*

acknowledgements

For their help and encouragement, I am grateful to Kate and Roy Link, Fred Rogger, and Joanne White. Thank you also to Kathryn Mulders, who read the first draft and offered her insight. This novel would not be were it not for Ann.

chapter one

The Community Corrections office occupies the upper floor of a concrete building, its midriff trimmed with green tiles like a gaudy belt, circa 1977, when it butted into the oldest part of town. The neighbouring clapboard and shingled homes date from the late 1890s. Picture sweaty saddle horses dozing with reins looped over the gatepost, hear cream-rimmed bottles clinking in a cart, smell the cattle, fresh milled lumber drying, sawdust in the air. The claim is that it was a simpler, perhaps more innocent era. Silver maples and weeping willows newly planted then to fend off the frontier dust of Interior British Columbia are now three feet thick at their base and finally shading the yards dreamed by the pioneers. Except now the neighbourhood has gone to hell. Even twenty-odd years faded, the crass newer building intrudes here, along with its unpleasant business. Clients loiter on the sidewalk out front, or sit on the curb smoking cigarettes, sometimes fishing stubs from the ashtray by the door. Always loafing, waiting for a ride to show up or a half-clear decision to hit them, in soiled jeans, all too often looking their part, that of criminals.

Upstairs with his swivel chair turned toward the window, a smoked glass shield, the probation officer's eyes meander. Across the street, among the tended yards and gardens, up the gravel alley, padding like a tomcat at a distance, peeking into open porches and off-kilter sheds. Ordinary domestic scenes have come to instill a peculiar mix of envy and suspicion in him. Something of an occupational hazard, as well as the fallout from his own circumstances over the past eight months or so.

The telephone rings.

"Peter Ellis," he answers, listens, pulls a grey metal drawer, selects the legal-size file in question, opens it on his desk, reaches for a pen, and jots notes in the running record. "I see. Can I ask your name? Well, this information should go to the police, and they may want to get in touch with you. All right, I understand, and I will follow up. But without a witness the police won't charge him, you realize? No, it's very helpful. I don't mean to pressure you. Sure, give it some thought. Thank you."

Mid-morning and someone has made another pot of coffee. Peter can smell it, and he rises from his chair, drawn by instinct and addiction to the Colombian brew.

As a former student of literature and lower-case communist who once attended rallies and freely signed all manner of petitions, he had never had any interest or intention of getting involved in the *Justice System*. When he first began working as a probation officer, a few of his friends questioned the move, and thereby his values. With these keen defenders of human rights he took an almost apologetic tone, claimed the job was a trial run, just a means of survival, certainly temporary. He chews gum at a range of paces, aggressively at the moment, while he swivels back and forth in his chair, prioritizing the work at hand. What he didn't admit to anyone, even to himself for a long time, was that this job hooked him immediately. Every day it places him at the crisis point in someone's life, tangent to a stupid mistake, a rage, an arrest.

In the beginning each crime is new: petty theft, a pensioner hobbling away with a frozen Cornish hen in her purse; auto theft, a car chase that ends in a crash, with one teen in hospital and another in jail; impaired drivers after every weekend; welfare fraud, low-brow credit scams; sexual offences, historical incest come to light; uttering threats, and spousal assault. After almost two years in the business, Peter has dealt with each of these and their variants many times, dozens, hundreds altogether. Common elements of local crime: alcohol, unemployment, ever lurking lust and anger. In this town there are rarely convictions for white-collar transgressions, the recent exception being a pharmacist busted for trafficking pills, with an interesting list of customers. Mostly it unfolds after dark, the offshoot of a noisy night in the bars, the ugly blossom that stems from years of toxic social compost.

Peter shies from judgment, despite or maybe partly to spite his Baptist upbringing. He suffers with imagination like vertigo lately, glimpsing life's infinite heartbreaking scenarios. He wonders whether it is some errant part in himself, some piece askew, that enables his rapport with the probation clients, the offenders.

He turns to his computer, enters one of his numerous required passwords, and spends the mandatory time to scan and delete various emails, weeding out the ones to which he must respond. Then he turns to the physical files stacked upon his desk, all in need of an update — warning letters for missed appointments, collateral phone calls, and the never-ending breach reports requesting a warrant.

When clients reporting in can't remember his name, when the administrative assistant asks who their PO is, they refer to him as *the guy with the hair*. He has a thick shock, dark when cut close, but copper-coloured and unruly in its current length. Beneath this and a tall brow, his eyes are grey, his face long and slightly crooked. An oval button-size birthmark hangs below his left eye, so seen from that side he looks a bit like a sad mime.

The central part of the office is a maze cluttered with equipment — printers and photocopier, fax machine, partitions, tables and shelves laden with stacks of forms and files in transit. The individual offices all open off this space; the two administration staff work in a cross-fire of voices.

George Woodgate, the manager, is six foot seven, head and shoulders above the partitions, so he can stand in his doorway and direct his gravelly commands wherever he likes. He's a former prison director who moved to this community supervision office en route to retirement. Woodgate and his wife found themselves a tidy property in a rural neighbourhood, and he likes the region for all the fishing and hunting it offers. In the prisons both inmates and employees are identified by surnames, and Woodgate has retained the habit, as well as his steel-grey hair in a brushcut. The manager pronounces Ellis more like *Alice*, which Peter suspects is intentional because he seems to be often out of favour with the man.

"*Alice!*" the call comes, and a few heads duck slightly while hands finger keyboards.

Peter feels the administrative assistant's eyes following him because she relishes these little scenes in the manager's office. He steps in to face the marching music. Woodgate sits ramrod straight in his treasured leather chair with a document in hand, which he plops on the desk to launch things. No pleasantries.

"We have a couple of questions concerning this pre-sentence report, the fraud charge against Gauthier. We, meaning Judge Vanderkraan, and me. Questions I couldn't answer when he telephoned a few minutes ago."

The managerial glower is about as fierce as any Peter has seen. Judges are sometimes critical of PSRs in court, especially peeved by inaccuracies of a hurried probation officer, but Peter hasn't heard of one actually calling Woodgate to make the point. This doesn't seem like good news, and he shifts his feet.

"Number one — how can you justify recommending a discharge on the sole condition of restitution, which is a fraction, about *one-third*, of the amount of her fraud?"

"Well —"

"Ah!" Woodgate raises his gorilla-length index finger. "Number two — *how do you justify a discharge in the first place?* This is fraud. Have you heard of the concept of minimum sentences? Well, check the Criminal Code, Alice. People can do federal time for fraud. A discharge is hardly an option in this case, and the judge wasn't pleased when the halfwit defence requested one, anyway, and pointed out your bleeding-heart recommendation."

Peter knows enough to let the wind subside before he ventures a reply. "Well, Ms. Gauthier was only working part-time while on welfare. If she had declared the income, she would've still received social assistance, just not as much. So I subtracted the amount she had the right to from the total, which left seven thousand or so as restitution."

"Nice to know you're a math wiz," Woodgate barks, at which the administrative assistant snickers from behind.

"Even that amount would take her years to repay. They lost the family farm in Manitoba. So they moved out here and her husband got a job on a logging crew, but then he had an accident, and Workers' Compensation won't —"

"Please!" Woodgate raises his hands to his big ears in mock horror, rubbing his crew cut. "This world isn't fair. Get over it. We aren't social workers, Alice. You might have heard me say that before?"

Yes, thinks Peter, *and it's usually a sign the rant is concluding.*

"The woman committed an indictable offence. In future don't be pushing for social revolution in your reports, especially when it embarrasses a judge."

Peter shakes his head. "Oh, absolutely not."

Woodgate cocks his head, a possible indication that any impertinence might warrant an old-fashioned flogging.

"I mean," Peter adds, "that was never my intention. It was an oversight … not checking the Code."

"That's what I told Judge Vanderkraan — that it was the mistake of an *auxiliary* officer of the court." Woodgate tosses the report into his shredding basket and turns to other business on his desk without lifting his gaze to Peter. "That will be all … for the moment."

chapter two

Next Monday morning Peter swipes his card through the MAG-ID screen at the rear entrance of the building. Somebody's cigarette has been left smouldering in the steel ashtray beside the door, nicotine going to waste, but he denies a wacko urge to stop for a puff. He mutters at the time displayed by the ID screen and hauls open the metal door. The system was installed last year, supposedly for security reasons, but it neatly logs the entry and exit of employees, their time, in other words. Tardiness was never a problem for Peter until Karen left. She always set their alarm clock. He lived, and for the most part thrived, on her time. Since her departure, Peter has struggled to keep both oars in the water, never mind spring out of bed in the morning. His head holds a dull ache like a bruised apple, and he craves the pills stashed in his desk.

He detours through the office kitchen to grab a coffee and hopefully evade notice by the admin. A film of sweat is already on his forehead — one of those mornings. Cup in hand, he slips past the file room.

"Good morning, Pete!" the admin sings out in her stinging, high-pitched voice of horror on a Monday morning.

"Ah, morning, Tammy," he concedes, approaching the table abutting her desk where documents are lined up. Three bail intakes, fallout from an average weekend. Peter studies the undertakings issued by the police and the justice of the peace, sips his coffee, before turning to face the three persons across the counter surnamed Charlie, Gilson, and Nolin. Ms. Gilson's UTA is clipped to an active probation file; Mr. Charlie is an old-timer who gets his cowhand's pay once a month and lands in jail every two or three; the other, Nolin, is unknown, arrested on five charges, which isn't an all-time high, but noteworthy.

Peter steps up to the counter. The three of them are seated as far apart as possible in the worn chairs of the waiting room. "Good morning. Sorry to meet under these circumstances. I'm the bail supervisor, Peter Ellis, and you've been directed to report to this office."

Raising his mug, he steadies his arm with effort and takes another essential sip of coffee. He meets the smiling eyes of old Levi Charlie, slouched in the corner, with a purple bandana knotted around his dark neck. Ms. Gilson looks forty aping seventeen. Already on probation for the theft of some guy's wallet, over the weekend she was arrested for assault on another fellow. She's the sort of client male probation officers will *not* interview in private for fear of allegations. In this case Peter has an easy way out. Not so, unfortunately, with the beefy young jock stepping forward to face him across the counter.

"Listen, I'm already late for work. I'll come back later on my lunch hour. See you then." The man swivels for the door, his silver glow-in-the-dark sneakers squeaking on the linoleum.

"Ah, Mr. Nolin?" Peter says. "It's not quite that simple. Please have a seat and I'll be with you as soon as I can. Ms. Gilson, because you're already on probation, I'll let your PO know you're here and she'll deal with your undertaking. Levi, you old hellion, come on in." Peter holds open the security door as the dignified fellow enters in his worn cowboy boots, restraining his amusement.

"Hey, what's going on? I was here before him. I just told you I'm late for work!" Nolin thrusts his chest over the counter. "Old Tonto can wait. He's not going anywhere."

"This isn't a restaurant, Mr. Nolin. The business with this gentleman will take only a few minutes. When we're finished, then it's your turn. You're facing a number of serious charges, which will take time to process. You might want to call your workplace and let them know you'll be late this morning." Peter feels hair rising on his neck, an instinctive male heat in his chest and upper arms. He compensates by lowering his voice almost to a whisper. "Of course, you're free to go. No one's stopping you. I'll call the police and let them know you're in breach of bail. They'll arrest you again, and I'll recommend you be held in custody until your first hearing in court next month. Or you can sit down and shut up."

This last phrase casts a sudden silence over the office, the admin's fingers momentarily suspended in air, since she has never heard this tactic used so bluntly before, or certainly not by Peter Ellis. Another PO, Greg Milchem, looks up from the photocopier with an amused gleam for conflict in his eye. The security door has closed. Peter holds papers in both hands but is squared off across the counter from Nolin. Old Levi Charlie stands at the side of Tammy's desk, his mouth a gentle wrinkle. He winks at her when she glances up.

Levi's face is lined like old dark leather, darker than most of his people, the Secwepmc First Nation, also known as Shuswap. He stands more than six feet, a bit stooped as a result of fracturing and later breaking his spine, both times thrown from the same Brahma bull. The bull, with the registered name of Vaquero Vex, but known as Double V, retired from the national rodeo circuit twenty some years ago. The same year Levi did. They had a running contest for a few seasons, but their last ride was in Medicine Hat in 1979. Levi was transferred from there to Vancouver by ambulance, and two months later, home to Canoe Creek on the train with a nurse attending him. None of the doctors expected he would ever walk again, but the next spring he pulled himself up in the saddle and never lacked for work in the region. The ranchers liked to joke that the Indian was always the best cowboy around.

Peter and Levi make their way through the outer office toward the bail supervisor's desk, the latter knowing the way as well as the former does, having much more personal experience with the justice system over the past forty years. They reach Peter's desk, and he puts his cup down, feeling almost ill-mannered. "Coffee, Levi?"

The rodeo rider nods twice for emphasis. Peter goes to the kitchen, fixes a cup, black with the three sugars he knows Levi prefers, and grabs a couple of doughnuts out of a box somebody brought in. Then they sit and sip coffee and eat their doughnuts while Levi scans the morning newspaper. Peter waits and enjoys the silence. A bit of filtered morning sunshine. In fact, Levi could have signed papers at the counter and been on his way. But Peter has come to enjoy the man's company every two or three months, usually on Monday morning, charged as a result of getting drunk the former

Saturday night, more or less. Try as he might, Peter can't see the crime in that.

"Any salmon in the river yet?" he asks after a while.

Levi turns his chin up, considering the question. "A few. Run's just startin'."

"Are you training horses?"

Levi inclines his head with a faint smile. "Yeah, a few colts. They keep me in trainin'."

"I guess." Peter smiles, mainly in wonderment. Levi's date of birth is listed as 1948–03–01. The month and day being estimates, because he was born with the deer, all according to his dear bygone mother. "So, ah, you were drinking again? Saturday night?"

"Yeah."

"Says here maybe you assaulted a server at the bar?"

"Assaulted, or *insulted*? Yeah, maybe I insulted him."

"Levi?"

"What? He grabbed my arm, so I grabbed his arm, he goes down. He insulted me first." Levi gently fingers his purple bandana and squints.

"I see." Peter sips his coffee and can't quite restrain another smile.

Fifteen minutes later Peter escorts Levi Charlie back through the office and bids him farewell. Levi loudly replies that he'll bring in a smoked salmon next time, with a wink, knowing full well the suggestion is a conflict of interest with justice.

Peter holds the waiting room door open and turns his attention to the unknown. "Mr. Nolin, thanks for your patience. Please come in."

"About time."

Peter leads the way toward his office once more. As they pass the admin desk, he catches an almost silent exchange with his peripheral vision. Nolin has made a face or gesture that elicits a faint snort from Tammy, a blushing smirk and bowed head when Peter glances back. *Those two mocking him?* It's a small town, and they're acquainted somehow, he guesses. Nolin is wearing loose synthetic warm-up pants currently in style as casual wear, and the material swishes with his swagger.

"Please have a seat." Probation Officer Ellis nods toward an empty chair as he sinks into his own and swivels to pull open a drawer stocked with blank forms. Focus on the task, no call to combat. Yet that primal sense is on full alert. "Where is it you work? Did you get a chance to call your employer?"

Todd Nolin slouches back, covers his face with his hands, rubs his eyes, combs his fingers back over his close-cropped scalp, then lets out an angry snort. "Hey, let me ask you something. Have *you* ever spent a night in jail?"

"No," Peter lies without compunction. As a matter of fact, he did spend one night in a scary cell in Mexico long ago, but he's not about to play truth or dare with this guy. Nolin's eyes are expressive, yet hard to read: measures of hostility and arrogance, but also of entitlement and an almost forlorn appeal. He's been so hard done by getting arrested and all.

"I didn't think so. Well, it's not something I want to advertise, *Mister* Peters, okay. So let me sign whatever little papers you have there, so I can get down to the store."

"Ellis."

"What?"

"My name's Ellis. Peter Ellis. Not Peters."

"Whatever. Fucking pardon me. Can we get on with it?"

"All right, sure. Where is it that you work? Sorry to repeat myself." Peter carefully selects one pen, his favourite for the moment, from a holder full on the desk. "But that information's required for this little form."

Nolin's eyes smoulder, furious that he has to submit to civil process. "I'm the assistant manager at BBG."

"BBG? Is that the full name?"

"Blades, Boards, and Gear, the sports shop," he recites, as if he's giving directions to a deaf old man, as if this bureaucrat dude is so clearly uncool and out of the loop.

Question by question, they complete the intake form in a few minutes. Peter saves an obvious one for last, since it always leads into a review of the conditions of bail. "Residential address? Where will you be living?"

"Arbour Villa. That's why the cops sent me to talk to you, so I can go home."

"Maybe you've misunderstood. Your bail order, issued by a justice of the peace who acts on advice from the police and the prosecutor, prohibits you from being within one hundred yards of Arbour Villa."

"Yeah, yeah, but *you* can give me permission. It says right on there."

"That applies in some cases, rare ones. Not in yours, I'm afraid, given the seriousness of the charges you face. Which brings us to the order itself."

"Wait a second! All my clothes and stuff. That's where I live, so what am I supposed to do?"

"Find other accommodation," Peter says flatly. Before Nolin can start again he adds, "You've been charged with the following — assault causing bodily harm, sexual assault, unlawful confinement, possession of a restricted weapon, and resisting a police officer. The conditions of your bail order are as follows. 'Report to a bail supervisor' … today before four, it says, which you've done. 'And thereafter as directed.' I'll give you a slip for the next appointment before you leave. 'No contact or communication directly or indirectly with Marina Faro.' That means no phone calls or notes, no messages through a third party. 'Not to be within one hundred yards of 465 Arbour Street, except with prior written permission of the bail supervisor.' We've already covered that. And you're not permitted anywhere near your former residence. 'Abstain absolutely from the consumption of alcohol or non-prescription drugs and submit to breath or urine tests upon the demand of any peace officer who has grounds to believe you have consumed alcohol or drugs.' Self-explanatory, right? Also, Section 145.3 of the Criminal Code stipulates that anyone who doesn't abide by the conditions of an undertaking can be charged with breach of bail, which is an additional charge punishable by fine or jail. Do you understand the conditions of your order?"

"This is bullshit! She made the whole story up. She wigs out, then the old bat neighbour calls the cops and suddenly I'm on the wanted list, like O.J. Simpson or somebody. Fuck!"

"Do you understand the conditions of your order?" The jock's self-comparison almost amuses Peter — the excuse he's heard a hundred times before. "You've been arrested and are under investigation for an offence, actually five offences, but you may or may not be guilty. Do you understand the conditions?"

"Yeah, yeah! How do I get some clothes and my razor? That's what I'd like to know!"

"I'll contact Ms. Faro and ask her to gather those items for you. You can check back with me in a couple of days."

"Oh, I like that. Great service! Tell her I want my workout bag, too, and all my shoes, and the store stock catalogues from last week." He grasps his big square head in his hands. "Are we just about done here?"

"Soon. I need to take your photograph … if you don't mind standing there against that height strip on the wall."

Peter pulls a Polaroid camera from the desk drawer. Oddly enough, Nolin does as he's asked, although muttering under his breath. Some clients refuse to have their photo taken, and a PO can't force them into it. But Nolin must be used to having his picture taken, gets a kick out of it maybe. He stands six foot three and glares at Peter through the camera lens.

"Now if you could please sign this reporting slip for Thursday —"

"You mean I'm coming in here twice a week!" He scribbles his name and throws down the pen.

"This week, yes," Peter says, wondering if Nolin shouldn't report daily, given the rage he's in. He admitted to no prior criminal record, which may or may not be true. Either way it means nothing if he ignores the paperwork and seeks out his victim again.

A few months earlier a guy named Kavanaugh did just that — walked from the probation office straight home to take after his wife again with the nearest weapon to hand, a vacuum cleaner pipe, and left her scarred for life. Peter still cringes recalling the case, though he did everything by the book, and Woodgate later made a point of telling him not to blame himself — shit happens. Every time one of these guys slams the office door a probation officer considers the chances, the probability, of some further, maybe final act of violence.

After the client leaves, Peter typically spends another twenty or thirty minutes completing the new bail intake. He reviews the forms, makes a note of any missing information to be filled in at the next report date. He begins the file's "running record," with a bare-bones summary of the interview and his impression of the accused, usually a single paragraph. In Nolin's case Peter fills most of a legal sheet with handwritten notes. The charges indicate far more than the run-of-the-mill bickering and tussle between a couple. Something pushed this guy into the crazy zone. This prompts Peter to call the Royal Canadian Mounted Police's Victim Services for more background.

"Glad you called, Peter," Maggie McConachie proceeds at her usual breathless pace, easily outstripping him five words to one in their weekly dialogues. She's good at her job, and Peter has learned to heed her advice. "This was a scary incident. I was petrified for that poor young woman. He held her captive in that apartment for over an hour after the police arrived. We took Ms. Faro straight to the hospital. She had awful bruises, possibly fractured ribs. Nolin didn't give himself up for another hour after he let her out. He had a handgun, for heaven's sake! The police didn't push him, mainly for fear of suicide apparently, though none of them were in any hurry to be busting into the place, I assure you. We haven't seen the likes of it in this town for a long time."

"They released this guy on *bail*? What more do you have to do to be remanded in custody these days?"

"My sentiments exactly, Peter. I think anyone else *would* have been held." She lowers her voice to indicate that what she's saying is off the record.

"What do you mean?"

"You know who he is, don't you? Todd Nolin. He was drafted by the Buffalo Sabres a few years ago and played for their farm team. He even played part of a season with Buffalo. He came back here about two years ago. Apparently, there's still an outside chance he could be recalled or picked by another team. Anyway, he's about the only local hockey star we've had since Dave Borchuk played for the Philadelphia Flyers back in the 1970s, with Bobby Clarke and Bernie Parent."

"Dave Borchuk?"

"You don't follow hockey, do you? Borchuk owns BBG, the sports store."

"Nolin works there."

"That's right," Maggie says. "Getting the picture? Nolin's the young blood, a local star, and they think he can do no wrong. Even if he is a brute. This isn't the first time the police have dealt with him."

"I've run him on CDS. He doesn't appear to have any record."

"No, but years ago — he must've only been seventeen or eighteen — there was a hush-hush investigation. Others didn't think the victim's story held up, so nothing came of it. But I interviewed the girl involved."

"Aha! What was the charge?"

She sighs. "Sexual assault. Listen, I'll be sitting in on the next interview with Marina Faro, tomorrow or the next day. Some of these cops are about as tactful as pit bulls. Anyway, I'll fax it to you once it's been transcribed."

After they hang up, Peter takes another close look at the photograph attached to Nolin's file. Something in the guy's eyes gives him pause.

That same morning Peter picks a note from regional personnel out of his office mail slot: "Due to the current budget freeze no advanced training will be approved until further notice." His name remains on the eligibility list. He tosses the page into his recycling box with a nasty oath. It means he'll continue doing all the work of a trained probation officer, yet with no job security and for a fraction of the salary. Or will he? The local newspaper is looking for a reporter, but Peter can't quite see himself covering town council meetings and bowling tournaments. He might just file a grievance with the union, though he knows that stands a snowball's chance in hell of helping him.

A little later Woodgate calls out, "Alice?" and Peter drags his feet to the manager's office. He's got half a mind to challenge Woodgate on the training issue, especially since the man forecast such an easy progression through the ranks at the hiring interview. *But it's going on two years now, damn it!* Peter thinks. Of course, they've had the discussion before — three times, actually. Woodgate always waves his gorilla fingers in a helpless gesture toward the top of his bureaucratic pyramid, saying, "You know, the bean counters tell us … What can I say? It's out of my hands."

Yeah, Peter thinks now, but it saves this particular office some money, which looks great in Woodgate's year-end report.

"Your letter from personnel was copied to me," Woodgate informs Peter when he enters the manager's office. "Sorry to hear your training's postponed."

"Me, too," Peter replies curtly with all the challenge he can muster at the moment. Maybe he could get a job with the city in park maintenance or dog-catching or something.

"Stick with it and you'll get there," Woodgate mutters.

How motivational, Peter thinks, heartwarming really.

"Say, the young guy in your office a while ago, was that Todd Nolin?"

"Yeah."

"What's that all about?"

Peter provides a summary.

Woodgate shakes his head. "That boy was a good hockey player. It's a shame."

Peter isn't exactly sure what Big George means by this, nor, at the moment, does he give a shit. "I'd better get back to work."

"Right. That's all for now, Alice."

Peter returns to his desk, considering his lack of future. He ponders the scales of small-town justice where potential as a hockey star brings celebrity status, and in Nolin's case, entitlement to be an outright prick.

Slouching rebelliously in his chair, Peter props one heel on the windowsill. The news about his training, the lack thereof and the implications, has sapped his zeal for the job. An early lunch is in order, maybe a pint or two. But it's only five after eleven, so he's got at least a half-hour to kill. He clips his fingernails, mentally daring anyone to interrupt him. That takes three minutes, then he stares out the window for a while. Finally, he glances back at the documents and notes re Nolin on his desk. The victim's name and phone number catches his eye — Marina Faro.

At the first ring an answering machine clicks on. She's not taking any calls. No message on the machine, just a moment of static, then the beep. Peter states his name and reason for calling, recites the office number.

chapter three

After work Peter climbs into his rusty green Bronco and lights a cigarette, verging on a habit for him recently. Living alone, he rarely troubles to cook anymore. Whereas he used to faithfully prepare dinner for Karen and enjoyed that hour of the evening, he's become a regular in the frozen aisle and the deli section at Safeway, and this evening opts for chow mein and spring rolls.

It's a fifteen-minute drive home to a neighbourhood community that over many decades developed around a log-built roadhouse, dating back from when the highway was a wagon trail. Peter stops by the general store for a case of beer, since he drank a number last night and fears the stock is low. God forbid.

Approaching the house, he tries to ignore the condition of the place, now in its second season of neglect. The grass is long overgrown because he wasn't able to start the lawnmower come April, nor did he bother to get it fixed by the end of May. Dandelions are rooted and blooming yellow in the gravel driveway. The neighbour kids are out playing ball hockey again this evening as they have been for weeks since the National Hockey League playoffs began. He recalls the same boyhood tradition. They prop a sheet of plywood against the fence as a backdrop to their net, and for hours he hears the repeated whack of near misses and wild shots, big saves, and shouting. Peter sits at the kitchen island, eating chow mein, drinking beer.

Buying the house seemed a huge step at the time, for him and Karen, a decision weighted with all sorts of implications. Such as children. They considered two or three places that were barely more than cabins, with acreage in picturesque settings. Room for two, but no more. That was the reason they ended up in a fairly ordinary older house with four bedrooms, two baths, a full basement, a fenced backyard, and even a swing set waiting. Because they imagined children, cribs, toys, bicycles, and the required guest room for visiting grandparents.

For a while then they seemed almost prepared and stopped using birth control. Karen guided their positioning in bed. A few times she thought she was pregnant, and at first was disappointed when it wasn't so. Yet the last time the possibility appeared to cause her only anxiety. Peter picked up the test at the drugstore. The result was negative, and Karen was clearly relieved. Children never to be. He challenged her, which prompted a quarrel, one of the more serious he could recall. Looking back, it made more sense.

He's left with chow mein and beer, the house in disrepair, the cat rubbing against his leg starved for attention. And the sounds of the neighbour boys playing road hockey, the scrape of sticks, ball whacking plywood, and their carefree shouting.

Peter taught at the local college for a couple of years, mostly remedial English and upgrading courses. Only part-time, with nothing over summer months, and the chances of a full-time position were remote. So he was wide open to ideas, to anything short of telemarketing. Then he heard about the job with the probation office. Karen didn't like the idea. Socially conscious to a fault, she viewed the entire justice system as reactionary.

"Incarcerating people by the thousands is just plain medieval," she said. "I mean, apart from those who are truly a threat to society. The majority have mental health problems, disabilities, addictions — what possible good does it do to lock them away?"

"Well, it's called deterrence, I think —"

"It's called discrimination, too! Look at the percentage of prisoners who are aboriginal. It's something like twenty percent. And they make up less than three percent of the general population."

"I'm not defending that," he said in his own defence. "And I'm not signing on as a jail guard. It's community supervision, and it involves trying to help the same sort of people you're concerned about." He was excited about applying for the job, and a bit taken aback by Karen's reaction. Even then perhaps he missed a deeper level of significance in their different points of view.

And another thing: he didn't much like bringing home one-third of what she was earning. So pride played a part, but there was also significant personal debt to consider, the price of education. The work with probation was full-time, even if he was hired as an "auxiliary," therefore subject to layoff without notice. That didn't bother him — at first.

When he encountered former colleagues in the grocery store, the salaried college instructors, they sometimes asked how Peter liked his new position. Often with a quizzical tone, even raised brows, as though it were tough luck for him. He'd say just fine, thanks. His own answer always surprised him a bit by being true.

There was much to learn about the process of justice, from the paperwork to the principles of sentencing, punishment, and rehabilitation. And, for better or worse, probation — supervision of offenders in the community. Knowing where they live and hang out, their particular vices or tendencies, their histories on record. They bring in their crises and yellow-nail tragedies to discuss every month. The learning on the job is divided into sections and subsections, Peter has discovered, and as in reading the Criminal Code itself, he is easily sidetracked or lost.

Theft of oysters is his favourite obscure offence in the Criminal Code, Section 323. Living in a semi-desert a day's drive from the Pacific Ocean, he hasn't had to deal with an oyster shyster, aka pearl burglar. But he holds out hope, imagining he might share a peculiar bond with that person, man or woman, the serial shellfish thief.

He enjoys the writing the job entails — documenting interviews and discussions with clients, victims, police, and lawyers. Sometimes he's only a conduit of such paperwork, initials in the margins, but that's fine. There's been a flurry of requests for court reports of late, and Woodgate has started passing a few Peter's way. The manager was reluctant to do so because Ellis has no Corrections training, of course. But the other POs have more than they can handle, and after reviewing the rookie's work, Woodgate must have conceded to himself that an English degree counted for something, after all.

As junior employee, part of Peter's responsibility is supervision of persons on bail, awaiting their day in court.

Innocent until proven otherwise, they like to remind him, guys like that Kavanaugh, and now Nolin. After reading the police reports, the circumstances, or "circs" in office lingo, it's not easy to put them out of mind, standing face to face with a man who reportedly molested his own daughter, or one who beat his wife, then placed the shotgun muzzle between her legs and made his threats explicit. The authority of Corrections over bail clients is limited. Yet the immediate risk of reoffending is often greater; because the wounds are fresh, the offenders can still smell blood.

The telephone rings thirty or forty times each day. After thousands of calls, Peter has standardized his answer: "Peter Ellis speaking …"

A brief pause. She gives her name, returning his call. Late Tuesday afternoon.

As her voice registers, it prompts a subtle shift within Peter's beleaguered mind. A leap of memory to childhood: bird calls, the trickle of a forest stream. His imagination reaches out like this lately; his senses are craving.

"Ms. Faro, I work for Community Corrections." He drops his foot from the grey windowsill. "As the police may have informed you, Mr. Nolin's been released on a bail order and is now under my supervision. One of my responsibilities is to contact you, to make you aware of the conditions of his bail, and answer any questions you might have, hear any concerns." He repeats this all by rote, suddenly too conscious of his own dry words.

"Questions … concerns?"

"Yes, I realize it's been a difficult weekend."

"Difficult," she whispers, more to herself than the stranger on the telephone. "Well, *my* concern is whether he'll kill me like he threatened. That's the first question. Can you answer that?"

Her voice has a firm hold now on his attention. He notes nothing as simple as sarcasm or even bitterness. The hushed sincerity of what she's said startles him. He straightens in the chair. Strangely enough, no victim has ever put it to him quite this way. What can — how does he respond? She's waiting.

"No, of course, I can't," he says. "But I do want to assure you that your safety is our priority concern. That's why I called."

"Okay," she breathes into the phone, "thank you."

Every time she speaks his own response is delayed, like that of a robot with a faulty language sensor. Or a man grown wary of words. This time he delays so long that she hangs up, apparently thinking their business is finished, and he's left listening to his own thoughts and the dial tone.

chapter four

In some cases, such as with suspected sex offenders, one condition of bail is that the accused live in a residence approved by a probation officer, which then requires a home visit. Peter has this task on his agenda the next morning, so he signs out a Jeep and writes out the offender's name — Martin — and the address where he's headed on the whiteboard. Number 16 in a trailer park beside the railway tracks, about the lowest rent in town, and mostly paid via welfare. He's been there before to see other clients.

The sky is hazy with smoke from not-so-distant forest fires, sunlight tinted grey, and the air gritty with dust scattered by the trucks rumbling to and from the nearby mills. Trailer 16 has settled into the gravel and weeds over twenty years, the green aluminum faded and warped by seasons. The yard space is a tangle of weeds and cast-offs — a vinyl-and-chrome chair with broken legs, the skeleton of a child's bicycle. The add-on wooden steps wobble under Peter's weight as he draws a breath and firmly knocks. He holds the Martin file in the other hand at his side, the documents of authority enclosed.

Peter hears slow steps, the squeak of handle and hinges, greeted by a mumble, and the door left open while the man retreats inside. He follows, putting off his next breath, the stale air fetid. Martin has two previous convictions for sexual interference with children, and there have been other investigations yielding insubstantial evidence. The man is fifty-seven years old. His victim profile is prepubescent girls, in all cases from dysfunctional homes, neglected, easy prey to his deviant kindness, too often unreliable as their own witnesses. But the case under way looks clear-cut so far, and if convicted, Martin is looking at a few years in jail, federal time. The man now leans against the counter, limbs like sticks, his belly oddly distended, taking in the visitor with a murky, bitter gaze.

No conversation to speak of. Peter reiterates the conditions of Martin's bail, the mandatory *visit*, while noting to himself the meaning formed from contradiction. He wouldn't be here otherwise. Every surface is filmed with grease and dust, every corner and crevice of the trailer. Wood panelling, brown paint. With Martin's nod and a grunt for consent, Peter walks down the narrow hallway, briefly glancing in the rooms for anything obvious to flag concern. There's no expectation to look under the bed or start rooting through boxes, fortunately. And if he does spy a stash of adult porn, it may be noteworthy, but it's not against the law. There are no signs that Martin is a heavy drinker, nor are there firearms or strange tools lying around. In one corner of the living room, near the worn-out recliner padded with towels, are several framed photos on the wall.

"Who are these children, Mr. Martin?"

"Grandkids," he says, rubbing his chin. "Haven't seen them for years, since … since all this business began."

The photos do appear fairly old, slightly faded. "By this business, are you referring to your convictions for sexual interference in 1997 and 1999?"

He sneers wearily. "Yeah. All that, sure, the tapestry of justice. And my daughter didn't buy it, neither, but her husband does. So I talk to her maybe twice a year, never to the kids."

"That must be difficult," Peter says with a modicum of compassion and a degree of disgust. "Thank you for your co-operation. I'll see you at the office next week."

"Sure, you bet, Officer."

Back in the Jeep, Peter jams the file into his leather case. Despite the smoky haze and roving dust, he unrolls both front windows to let the rush of air rid him of Martin's smell and dark aura. There is no typical sex offender. Some are obsessively clean, but others, it seems, are almost anti-hygenic, living in littered hovels, the material reflection of their minds. Peter shudders and exhales. Instead of heading straight back to the office, he drives north past the mills, past the city limits, until he can peer into the gorge where the creek runs toward the river, the spring high water. He pulls off the road and takes in the view for a few minutes, leaning out the window, hoping the wind will help air out his mind.

There's a second file in his bag, on Nolin, that he brought along on impulse, thinking he might have time to swing by the victim's residence and give her a copy of the bail document. Usually, it's mailed out, or it's picked up at the office. But his brief conversation with Marina Faro has stayed with him, the nature of her voice. He'd like to offer her some reassurance, if possible, and he's curious.

The Jeep wends its way through town, and Peter pulls into the Arbour Villa parking lot. From the Nolin file he takes a manila envelope in hand, opens the door, and swings himself out. The building is clad with green-stained wooden siding, and he follows the sidewalk along in front.

A woman is bent over in the bordering flower garden. Although her back is toward him, she straightens at his approach, turns, and he's surprised by the age in her face yet the firm way she blocks his advance toward unit 5. She steps onto the concrete with a pronged garden tool upraised as though to parry the envelope in his hand. "No visitors today, sorry," she says.

"I'm just delivering this," Peter explains. "It's important that Ms. Faro receive it."

She studies his clothes, the hair curling over his collar, and raises an eyebrow. "Are you a policeman?"

"No." He balks at much more explanation to this woman but doesn't want to be rude. He notes the tended soil around the flowers and shrubs. "You have a very nice garden going here."

"I'm the caretaker, my husband and I, for nine years now," she says as though wary of his compliment, alert to any tactic and the envelope in his hand. She glances briefly past him, then back over her shoulder at unit 5 where the curtains of both front windows are drawn. "What brings you here?"

"To deliver this," he repeats, waving the envelope, ready to retreat.

"But what's your job?"

She wants to nail him down, and now it seems he can't escape without some explanation. "I'm a probation officer. My name's Peter Ellis."

The woman nods, outright scowling at him now. "So it's about that trouble on Saturday." Her raised voice reveals the trace of an accent he can't identify. "That young man's in jail now where he belongs!"

Her statement is incorrect, by lack of information, and this raises a bit of a dilemma for Peter. On the one hand, he's obliged to protect Nolin's confidentiality as best he can, though his release on bail is, in theory, public knowledge. On the other hand, given that Nolin is prohibited from being within three blocks of the complex, the caretaker is an ideal watchdog, so to speak, especially if she knows about the condition. Then there's the fact that one of her tenants went on a rampage in the apartment next door to her own, held his girlfriend hostage, forced a police standoff, and caused havoc for everyone in the building for several hours last Saturday night. She's got a right to her feelings, and maybe some explanation.

"As a matter of fact, ma'am, he's not in jail. He's been released on bail under certain conditions, and part of my job is supervising him."

Her face freezes for a moment. "How can you let him go like that? After what he did here, and what he did to her?"

"I share your concerns. He's facing a number of serious charges in court, but at the moment he hasn't been proven guilty, so he can't be held in jail."

"Prove what? I saw it all. The judge can talk to me. I heard the proof that night, and I listened to it for months before that." She glances again at the curtained windows of unit 5. Then she gestures at him to follow, leads him along the walk in front and up the steps to where her own door stands ajar. She leaves her garden clogs on the landing.

Once standing on the inside mat, he can see her floors are spotless, so he's faced with taking his own shoes off, and he's not sure about this meeting she's called. "I really should get going."

"I'm making coffee, a cup for you," she says in a persuasive manner, so he slips his shoes off and takes the chair she pulls out for him. Her name is Fay Kubova, she offers. Her husband's name is Juri, and he's lying prone in an armchair in the next room, lying very still but apparently breathing.

"This has always been a quiet complex, stable tenants, usually older people, some retired. They never have problems with their rent, never any noise. Until that couple moved in." She points at the wall her unit shares with number 5. "I spoke with her the very first weekend. Their party kept me awake until three, and I was over there knocking on the door at nine. Finally, she opened it, standing there barely dressed, and I gave her a piece of my mind. At least she had the decency to apologize, even when it wasn't her fault. Because she couldn't stop that … that monster. It happened again and again."

According to Fay, she would have never rented the place to the young couple in the first place, or else they would have been evicted after a month, had it not been for the fact that Juri knew that Todd Nolin had played in the NHL. This gave him status in Juri's eyes. The old man has followed the game since defecting to Canada nearly forty years ago. He roots for the Czechs, his countrymen, whatever team they play for.

"And he's mostly deaf," she points out, looking briefly at her inert husband in the other room. "So the noise never bothers him the way it does me. And it was getting worse, even on weeknights. So I got fed up, and I gave them a written warning two weeks ago."

"Sounds like they've caused you some grief," Peter says.

"Grief? Yes, *he's* caused grief, all right, mostly for that poor girl," Fay fumes, plunking a mug of dark coffee in front of him.

She sets out sugar and cream. Then she sits down, fixes her eyes on him, leans across the table, and tells Peter what happened.

Juri was watching the hockey game, sipping his third beer against the doctor's orders, oblivious to anything else.

Next door they were watching the game, as well. Several vehicles were crowded into the parking lot. Male voices and laughter, cheers and jeers boomed through the kitchen wall, and Fay wasn't happy about it. She finished the dishes, tidied up the kitchen, and considered marching over to complain.

"They're having another party next door," she informed Juri, moving over the carpet into his line of vision far enough to get his attention.

"What?"

"There's a party next door," she repeated, raising her voice over the announcer's commentary blaring from their own television. "Between this, and them, I can hardly hear myself think!"

"It's the playoffs!" Juri hollered as if she were standing twenty yards away. He craned his neck, not in anger but with the simple need to see the corner of the television screen her skirt was obscuring. The streak of a rubber puck. Clearly, he thought his answer explained everything — the weather, the economy, the ungodly noise next door.

Fay bustled around a bit, madder by the minute, then finally got her garden overshirt out of the closet and stepped outside. The evening was warm and pungent with the scents of greening lawns, spruce and pine, all the vegetation, roots, and leaves awakening.

She walked around the yard, checking the coiled yellow yard hoses, picking up the odd piece of litter. Traffic on the street was more aggressive than on an average night. Everyone was in a hurry to get somewhere, like a hockey game party. She gathered a couple of tools from the aluminum garden shed, then criss-crossed the lawn in a vengeful campaign against any and all weeds. From inside the apartments she could still hear the roar of the televisions, and raucous cheers from number 5.

Herbicides weren't something Fay had much experience with. On that point she'd stood her ground against Juri, who had been inclined to spray with just about anything short of green paint to achieve a flawless lawn. But last summer he had done little at all in the yard. Now she could already see where the dandelions had seeded, and she imagined their lengthening white roots. Some were more than she could oust with her hand shovel.

Dusk crept up on the neighbourhood and Fay's yard. Finally, there came a great roar from within unit 5, signalling the end of the hockey game. Soon after, young men appeared on the front steps, each with a beer in hand, laughing and yelling at one another in foul language. When she spotted Todd Nolin, Fay straightened and stared across the lawn until he noticed her. He avoided eye contact and made some remark to his buddies, which scored a great laugh. Not long after that they all piled into their vehicles and disappeared, much to Fay's relief. She supposed young Marina was inside cleaning up after the louts.

Fay put her tools away and climbed the steps into her own apartment. There she found Juri asleep in his easy chair. Fay shut off the television. She roused him gently and supported him as he made his way to the bathroom to rinse his dentures and prepare for bed.

"Who won?" she asked, then regretted the question.

He mumbled irritably, and she guessed he didn't know, that he'd fallen asleep before the game's end. This would trouble Juri greatly, and Fay did her best to prevent such embarrassment for him.

After he was settled in, she returned to the kitchen, plugged in the kettle, prepared the coffee maker for the morning, and set out the box of wheat biscuits. Once the water boiled, she fixed her nightly cup of Ovaltine, a thirty-year habit. Fay took her drink into the living room and was seated in her chair just in time for the ten o'clock news. She trusted the anchorman, admired how his voice portrayed all the grief and disaster he was given to cover. Sometimes she wondered what he did when the program concluded, and if he ever had a problem sleeping. As for Fay, she made her way to the bathroom, where she changed and washed, applied facial cream, and then went to bed.

She awakened later with a start, fumbled for her glasses, saw that it was almost 3:00 a.m. A horrendous crash and roar was coming from the next apartment. She rolled out of bed, grabbed her housecoat, and hustled downstairs.

Something smashed against the wall, something fell and was dragged or kicked aside. For a moment the voices were muted by struggle, then a short, vicious oath, then a wail. Then words and fragments blasted through the wall.

"They're laughing at me! Laughing, you slut! You want a good laugh, here —"

"Oh, dear God," Fay whispered, pacing back and forth from her kitchen to the walk-in closet at the end of the hall, trying to track whatever was going on. The girl screamed.

"Fucking little bitch …"

"Todd! *Pleeease!*"

Another crash, and a scramble of feet and objects

overturned. A prolonged wail, a series of cries, and pounding steps indicated that the girl was running upstairs. Fay turned and followed up her own stairwell, heard the man's steps thunder upward past her.

"Where do you think you're going?" a man's voice roared.

Fay tilted her ear to the wall at the top of the stairs, followed the girl's voice along to the upstairs bathroom, heard the door slam, frantic hands on the lock.

"Open the door!"

"Please, Todd!"

"Open this door, you slut!"

Fay was breathless. She heard a great thud against their bathroom door, then the crack and splintering. The girl's terrified sobs. It was less than two minutes since she awakened. Stricken with guilt for not acting sooner, she ran to the telephone and called 911.

Within five minutes there was a loud rapping at her own door, and Fay opened it to the alert concern of a young police officer. As she was explaining, she heard another officer knocking repeatedly at unit 5, and already a second patrol car was pulling in, its red and blue lights pulsing.

A window shattered. The young officer whirled away from Fay, one hand guiding her back into her apartment, the other unlatching his holster. The second officer backed away from the doorway of number 5, gun already in hand.

"Oh, dear God," Fay whispered, this time in earnest prayer.

chapter five

Returning every evening to the empty house, Peter is never sure which mood will greet him, but it's often on the darker end of the scale. Monday, Tuesday, Wednesday evening. His mind idly plucks at subjects to divert attention from the self and ponders the origin of *Wednesday*. After seven months, he misses the day's end conversations with Karen as much as anything, her presence in the kitchen, sitting at the island while he rinsed spinach in the sink, opening a bottle of wine, listening to the fluctuating tone of her voice, often a wry note. They talked about everything, so it seemed, including the creeping distance between them over the preceding year, without blame or much anger. But the leaving, when it happened, was still sudden and stark. The absence of her body, her face, her eyes, the understanding in her voice.

Fairly soon after she left he realized that almost all of his local friends were made through Karen, and along with her his connection to them was gone. He gravitated to isolation.

Only a couple of times since did he have any interest in other women, and he felt too awkward to act when the opportunities arose. Their few words shared were welcome, of course, and the invitation to call. One from a woman who once worked with Karen; they met briefly at some function. But even a visit is more than he feels prepared for yet.

Peter has got his newfound bad habits for company — cigarettes close to hand, drinking more than he ever has. A warm evening for May, Woden's Day. He sits on the back step with a smoke, a vodka tonic, and a can of beer. He tries to read, but every book he picks up lately seems either alien to him or too close to heart. Sometimes to combat the silence he plays music loud, mostly older stuff that he's had since before his marriage. Karen's taste was somewhat more varied, and she took every CD she ever purchased with her to California. She wasn't being mean-hearted, just a bit neurotic, he thought. Wasn't she starting afresh?

Anyway, he plays "El Corazon" by Steve Earle, and it feeds his needy sense of rebellion. The man's been married how many times, fearless heart and all? He went to jail on drug charges, for crying out loud, and wrote two albums behind bars.

Blame is pointless. One more drink drags him too near to self-pity. The neighbour kids are out playing ball hockey until their blond mother calls them in at bedtime, casting a glare in his direction. His own backyard is overgrown, grass matted, knee-high weeds gone to seed, everything dried out or wilted by the heat.

The hours have blurred, and well after ten the daylight lingers. Although he hasn't paid his subscription in months, the newspaper still gets delivered, a pile of back issues stacked by the door. For weeks the headlines have concerned the forest fires raging across the entire Northwest. The haze of smoke in the air gives an amber tint to the light that Peter finds unnerving — too much like urban smog threatening to smother the whole country.

He rises from the step and goes back into the house where thoughts of the past await him in every room. He's trapped in there and must live among them. The place has been for sale for six months, but the market is way down and there are no buyers in sight. But he has his memories ...

"Look at my feet," Peter said one day last November.

Karen did so, turning her head while brushing her teeth. She glanced down at his feet, undried and flushed from his shower, splayed before him on the purple bath mat as he sat naked on the edge of the tub.

"Uh-huh?" she mumbles, her mouth still full of toothpaste, checking her watch. He was like a sleepy child in the morning. This was a workday.

"Don't they look like animal feet?" he asked. "I mean, do you ever look at a part of your body and have this primal flashback to huddling in a cave, squatting in a forest or something?"

Karen bent to spit in the sink, laughing with the rush of tap water. She wiped her mouth, examined her hair in the mirror. "My own body or yours? Sweetheart, it's ten to eight. I've got a meeting first thing this morning, and I can't be late. You'll still have your feet tonight. We can study them then."

"Okay," he growled, reaching for his clean underwear. "Now you're talking."

Later that week, on Sunday morning, it happened. They had been together eight years, long enough that Peter could recognize the weight of an impending discussion by the way Karen spooned her muesli. Her hand moved too deliberately and hovered. Peter rose to top up his cup of coffee. He felt foggy, suddenly wary, outgunned by Karen's powers of concentration.

"There's something we have to talk about," she said with none of her usual irony, and his heart faltered.

What really threw him was how quickly Karen proceeded from that opening cliché to the kicker, from gambit to checkmate in a couple of minutes. She looked as beautiful as ever, tawny hair slightly dishevelled, yet her green eyes were evasive. Strangely calm.

Snow was steadily falling, the coffee was still fresh in their vintage beige enamel percolator, orange slices lay on a plate, images from a poem in memory. Peter had fried some bacon, three eggs, and a tomato, and with his Lea & Perrins was all set to savour a country squire's breakfast. Earlier they'd had a sleepy wake-up love session, and the note of her climax lingered in his ears. The final time.

"Is it the meat?" he asked, gesturing at his plate, appetite quickly fading. Reaching for any humour, even vegetarian, hoping for her smile, for that much reassurance.

"What?"

"The bacon. It stinks up the house, you always say. I try not to eat it very often, but I could go without. I could. Maybe there's a twelve-step program for bacon hounds."

She shook her head.

Her look hit him in the pit of his stomach. "Is it the Pink Panther thing? Humming that theme song, or my imitations of Inspector Clouseau? I'll stop. No more silly accents. I promise."

"No ..." She glanced down with a sad half-smile she couldn't help.

Her expression caused his heart and hope to stall, then tip into a perilous nosedive. After all, he knew the gist of what she had to say before the words came out. Details didn't really matter, because they excluded him. So at least he was relieved of guilt in that regard. She needed some time alone, freedom. She'd met someone via an on-line discussion group or chat room. Somebody from Crescent City, California. They had already had a rendezvous in Seattle, that weekend "conference" two months ago. Karen had asked for a leave of absence from the school, for now, but expected she would be giving her notice.

"You're serious?" He laughed, or attempted to laugh, but his face collapsed, words rolling out like miscast dice. "You have a pen pal in California? And now you're off to try living with him? Yes, okay, I get it. Wow! Is he like a beach surfer type, or software tycoon, or what?"

"She's an artist, a sculptor," Karen spoke softly, head down, her reference to gender escaping him at first with his hearing impaired by anger.

Peter had slept with Karen nearly every night for eight years, knew the shape of her body as he had once known his mother, even more intimately than that. He loved her, body and soul, and the first sense of impending separation was like free fall, a countdown to his own destruction. He couldn't imagine anything else that morning.

They had met while each was in their final year of university back east. Peter was six years older, having interrupted his studies to travel and bum around quite a bit: Mexico and the Mediterranean, then Thailand, one winter at a resort in the Rockies as a breakfast cook, skiing every afternoon. By contrast, Karen was intently focused on a teaching career and had job prospects even prior to graduation. They first met at an opening in a small gallery exhibiting the work of a painter who was a mutual acquaintance. For Peter the artist was an occasional drinking companion turned rival in the course of that night. Karen, it seemed, was a more special guest. Peter recalled the moment hearing her laughter behind him, a throaty, playful laugh that made his head turn. That was Montreal, *c'est la vie*. Later they shared a pot of mussels steamed with Pernod in a café on rue Saint-Denis.

Then Toronto. Karen's first job was in a suburban school north of the city, near her hometown where her parents still lived. Peter never hit it off with the prospective in-laws, a well-established family that made him feel like a drifter and gold digger. For three years in Ontario he worked as a tutor and did a few stints cooking in fine but ill-fated restaurants, now with an English degree. When Karen raised the idea of moving west, Peter leaped at it, and within a week purchased a van to transport their belongings — a faded green Econoline. It had gotten them across the country, the Prairies, Kicking Horse Pass, and for him more or less back home. Big, clean rivers and sagebrush on the side hills. Now it seemed the beautiful middle of nowhere.

"What about the cat?" he asked suddenly that fateful Sunday morning after several minutes of reflective silence. Karen still sat at the breakfast table, Anais rubbing against her legs. He had rescued the tabby from the SPCA as a birthday present for Karen.

"I was hoping she could stay with you for now," she said with her first hint of emotion.

Peter scowled, unreasonably pissed off by the suggestion. "Where?" he asked, on the offensive now, raising his arms wildly. "What about the house? You know I can't pay the goddamn mortgage alone. Am I supposed to advertise for roommates or what?"

Karen had her head down and was stroking the cat's back with her hand. "I'll contribute my share for the time being, of course. Perhaps we'll have to sell the house, and I'm very sorry if it means disrupting you. I don't think we should get into all this at the moment. Peter, this means a big adjustment for both of us. I'm sorry to take you by surprise like this —"

He cut her off with an angry wave, turning to the window to escape meeting her eyes. Fact was, though he had grown very fond of their place, all things considered he didn't really care about the house. Even bankruptcy seemed a minor inconvenience in the wake of her news that morning.

Peter stood with his arms crossed, staring out the window. Despite the sudden instability of his life, fresh snow brought to mind the possibility of skiing that day. He guessed the temperature to be about minus five to minus ten degrees Celsius, calling for blue wax, possibly green. For a moment this thought steadied his mind, gave him something tangible to consider: smoothing out wax along the base of the skis with the heel of his hand. Then he realized that Karen wouldn't accompany him skiing that day, and possibly never again. She had such aptitude and grace on skis, a naturally long stride and an eagerness for this same sport that Peter loved so much. He imagined her skiing, cutting a telemark turn on a slope of virgin powder, and he began to cry. The large snowflakes continued to fall, each one like a particle of his own hope, and soon his heart would be empty.

chapter six

A fusillade of unforeseen work hits Peter the next morning. Recently, a probation officer went off on maternity leave, and as yet they have no auxiliary to fill her position. Now the summer holiday rotation has begun, sometimes leaving the office short-staffed. Greg Milchem picks this day to call in sick. From the minute he steps in the door, Peter is taking phone calls from the police, social services, then some irate ex-girlfriend of an offender trying to track the man down for child support payments.

"I'm acquainted with him, yes. I'm afraid I can't give you his address. Or his phone number. I hear you, I tend to agree, but what you're asking for is confidential information. As a matter of fact, I can't even confirm that he's reporting to this office. That's your assumption ... That's one way to put it. Let me give you the number for Maintenance Enforcement."

The counter bell rings repeatedly throughout the

morning — clients to rebook, some three days or a week late, some half-drunk at 10:00 a.m. In between these varied tasks Peter attempts to update a few of his own ninety-odd files. This week's bail intakes are still in the admin basket, out of sight and out of mind for the moment, well down the priority list. Noon takes him by surprise, and he flees out the back door.

He fights the urge to smoke for all three blocks to the 7-Eleven, where he buys a pack. Then he goes to Frieda's Deli, ostensibly German, but which employs a Punjabi woman in the kitchen who makes terrific samosas. Afterward he makes his way along the sidewalk with another smoke, sucking a mint. Despite the ever-present haze and amber-tinted light, the town doesn't look so bad, even has a dusty charm.

When he arrives back at the office, shortly after one, Todd Nolin stands there scowling in the waiting room. Catching sight of him, Peter recalls that he hasn't yet made any arrangements about Nolin's personal effects.

"Todd is here to pick up his things," Tammy sings out. She's on a first-name basis with the jock, it seems, because as it turns out they attended the same high school in years gone by.

"Yeah," he snaps, "so where's my stuff?"

Peter stalls his reply, checking his mail slot, swallowing his mint before he turns to the front counter. "Hello, Mr. Nolin. I did speak with Ms. Faro the other day. She was still quite shaken from the events of the past weekend. Once we discussed the conditions of your order and so forth, it didn't seem the right time to ask her to gather your belongings. If you see what I mean …"

"No, I don't!" He jerks his big jaw sideways, an odd spasm of frustration, ill-concealed rage. It's very easy to picture him out on the ice, dropping his gloves, circling an opponent. "I need my clothes and all my shoes, and you said you'd have them here this afternoon."

"Tell you what," Peter says, "I'll call her again, once I get back to my desk, and see if I can pick up your things this afternoon. If that works out, I can save you the trip back here. I'll drop the stuff off at your workplace if you like."

"Yeah, sure," Nolin snarls, backing toward the exit, "with everybody at the store watching. No thanks. Just get it here and call me."

Peter finds the Nolin file-in-progress in the secretary's pending work basket, awaiting information entry for the Corrections Data System. He takes it back to his desk and drops it on top of the pile. Sometimes that's all it is — a heap of work waiting to be done. It's easier not to dwell on the fact that each file bears a name and concerns someone in crisis — victims, offenders, families falling apart. The circumstances of new files, which he receives via fax in the form of a narrative, have become all too familiar: a relationship on the rocks, man gets drunk, argument ensues, he shoves her, she shoves him, he slaps her, holds her against the wall, the bed. Someone calls the police. And Peter deals with the aftermath, does the paperwork, and makes the phone calls.

After three rings, he expects to leave another message, ready to note with his pen in the file's running record: "303-7131 message to call re TN's clothing, etc."

"Hello."

"Yes, Ms. Faro?" He jots the date in the margin column. "Peter Ellis calling from the probation office. We spoke the other day briefly. And I stopped by your place yesterday, in fact, to deliver a copy of the undertaking with Mr. Nolin's conditions of bail. But your neighbour, the landlady, discouraged that idea. And she was right. I shouldn't have come by unannounced."

"Yes, she mentioned you were here."

Again there's something in her voice, or the absence of something, that's unsettling. And a sound in the background — water dripping? Maybe she's washing dishes. What people do while they're on the phone always intrigues him. Are they typing sporadically, shuffling papers, digging in a drawer?

"How are you doing today?" Peter asks carefully, giving an opportunity if she wants to talk, but not wanting to intrude. He's not a counsellor and is wary of saying the wrong things.

"Oh, I'm okay, thanks," she replies, likely moving her other hand in the dishwater. "At least I feel better than I did yesterday, and a lot better than the day before that. Now I just need some sleep."

"I see. Has Ms. McConachie been in touch with you?"

"The police assistance worker? Yes, I've talked with her a couple of times. She seems nice. Actually, I'm meeting with her later this afternoon to review my statement."

"Maggie's great. We've worked together a fair bit, and things always go more smoothly when she's involved."

"Smoothly," Marina echoes.

Peter plainly hears the lapping of water as she shifts position. Is she in the bath? At 1:30 in the afternoon?

"That's an interesting choice of word," she says. "Not the first that comes to my mind, since Saturday night."

There, he said it — the wrong thing. Along with that, her elusive tone, and the fact she's in the bathtub, he feels himself freezing up. He can't do that again; he has to get to the point.

"No, you're right. I meant, given your difficult situation, and based on my experience with her in the past, Maggie seems to know. It's not just a job for her. She cares a lot about people."

"Yes, I get that feeling. I don't mean to bitch at you …"

"Hey, that's okay. I have a knack for putting my foot in my mouth."

"Really?" she snorts, sliding upright in the tub, it sounds like.

"Yeah, it seems. The reason I called is that Mr. Nolin asked me about obtaining some of his personal effects, clothing and so on. I don't want to trouble you, but would you mind packing some of his things?"

"And Bucko's going to pick them up?"

"No, no. He's not allowed anywhere near your residence — not within a hundred yards. If you'll help us out by gathering some of his clothes — and shoes, he made a point of saying he wants all his shoes — then if it's all right, I'll come by and pick them up."

"His precious shoes, of course. Okay, I'm glad to get rid of his shit. The sooner the better. When can you pick it up?"

"Anytime." He hears her rise out of the tub, water dripping, then the drain. "You mentioned you had an appointment with Maggie McConachie?"

"That's at three."

He checks his watch. "Is it too soon to come by within the hour, by two-thirty or so?"

"No, sure, see you then," she says, hanging up.

Some offenders Peter talks to in the course of a day lack communication skills and wield a phone like a blunt object. Others approach it like a blowhorn, bellowing demands, often without identifying themselves. When he asks the caller to do so, if only to make the point, a common response is: "It's me!" Anecdotal evidence of a crude egomania common to criminals. They make their excuses, complaints, swear vigorously, and hang up even if they don't get their way.

Lawyers, on the other hand, headline their names like magic words, *shazam*, schmooze a bit, then slip in their points, angling for information, or agreement as to what upstanding citizens their clients are at heart. Peter got hoodwinked a few times in the beginning, especially by women. He's decided that if he's ever in need of counsel he'll get a female lawyer, since he believes they have a natural aptitude for the profession — all the reading between the lines and other tricks of communication.

The victims in files he deals with, more often than not, are women. It's a bail supervisor's responsibility to contact them at least once. And it's common to have them call back frequently for different reasons; too often, though, they take it upon themselves to sort their messes out. They react in many different ways to their situations, he's learned, and may well have a hate on for men, understandably. Ms. Faro is a case in point.

After tidying up a few matters, he signs out one of the office Jeeps, grabs the keys, and exits down the back stairs to where the forest-green vehicles are parked three in a row. Exercise caution, son, his elder interior self warns, in any communication with such persons. Not all are women. Every few months there comes along a husband victim, the last one with umpteen stitches in his head from a waffle iron. Peter lets the engine idle for a few moments, rolls down the driver's window, then pulls out onto the street.

It's an afternoon in late May, gently humid. The trees are in bud, the grass becoming green. He imagines Karen in

California grilling vegetable kebabs for the sculptress on a cedar deck overlooking the Pacific, later having wild lesbian sex in the loft. Peter navigates the potholes and minimal traffic of the town streets. He's not sure what to think, what to feel, anymore.

Arbour Villa is located in a newer part of town where there are a lot of earth-tone accents to the homes and exotic shrubs. Nolin's standoff last Saturday night was no doubt quite an event for the neighbourhood. The apartment complex is neat and tidy, thanks to the efforts of the landlady, who is out there again, garden trowel in hand. By the time he reaches the sidewalk in front of the building, she has once more positioned herself in front of unit 5. She reminds him of a dignified, territorial old dog that scares off unwanted salesmen.

Peter smiles. "Hello, Mrs. Kubova. Ms. Faro's expecting me today. I spoke with her by telephone just a few minutes ago."

The old woman points the garden shovel at him, as if to say, "Stand still, boy." Then she goes up the steps and knocks on the door of unit 5. He notes that all the curtains are still closed.

After a moment, the door opens. The caretaker leans in quickly and whispers to her tenant.

"No, it's okay." Peter recognizes Marina Faro's voice from the telephone, then catches only an exchange of whispers.

Fay Kubova withdraws and comes sideways down the steps as though she's wearing a pair of skis. She studies Peter's face as she passes nearest him at the foot of the stairway. He goes up, and the young woman is standing with the door open, beckoning him in.

Peter nods as he enters. "Ms. Faro, I'm Peter Ellis from the probation office."

"Hello." She closes the door behind him.

He steps inside to get clear and nearly trips over two bulging nylon sports bags. Beside these is a large cardboard box heaped with shoes, mostly brand-new runners.

Marina stands in the kitchen with her arms crossed, wearing an oversize sweatshirt and loose black jeans, long dark hair still slightly wet. She gestures with her bare left foot at the bags. "There it is."

"Okay." Peter wonders about the box full of shoes. From the envelope in his hand he withdraws a copy of the bail document and extends it to her. "This is a copy of the undertaking given to Mr. Nolin. He's bound by the conditions listed there. Number two prohibits him from any contact with you. Number three prevents him from coming within a hundred yards of your residence."

"I see." She grips the paper for a moment, scanning the form and language as if they record a private transaction. And in a sense they do — a violent one. Then she holds up the document as though it were a piece of junk mail, her brows raised above expressive brown eyes. "How does this prevent him from doing anything?"

"Good point. *Prohibit* is a better word. If he makes contact with you, or comes near your residence, he'll breach the conditions set out by the court. He'll be arrested and charged again."

"But he's got what, four or five charges already? What's one more? What you're saying is he's out there and will do whatever he wants. Consequences don't mean a whole lot to Todd. Isn't that obvious?"

Peter hears her fear, her frustration with this interim justice and the photocopy in her hands. She places it on the counter by her telephone, shaking her head. An orange cat ambles sleepily into the kitchen, then freezes in stride, eyeing Peter as it twitches its tail.

"It's okay, Tiger. Did we silly humans wake you up?"

Marina leans over and scratches the cat behind the shoulders. As she does, with her weight on one knee and her other leg extended for balance, the line of her thighs and behind becomes a sinuous black denim curve. Her damp brown hair falls alongside her lowered arm. Her tone is playful with the cat, her mouth almost smiling. But as she raises her head Peter sees the purple bruise along her right cheekbone, and red marks on that side of her neck. He averts his eyes, avoids her glance. But she knows — too much, it seems. A new sense of anxiety ignites within him. He turns his attention to the overstuffed bags, the cardboard box.

"Mr. Nolin stressed that he wanted *all* of his shoes. He has quite a few of them, I see."

"Oh, yeah. He's got at least a dozen pair of runners, and he's got trainers for the gym, court shoes for tennis and squash, hikers, deck shoes, and a bunch of sandals. He gets them wholesale from the store and brings home a new pair almost every week."

"Really?"

She nods. "Todd never wears the same thing on his feet two days in a row. Sometimes he'll go home at noon just to change his shoes. It's a big deal with him."

"No kidding? Well, I'll load the shoes and this other stuff in the Jeep and be on my way." Peter stifles a grunt as he lifts the box. He calculates there must be twenty pairs, maybe three thousand dollars' worth of sporty footwear. It's a bit crazy.

Fay Kubova eyeballs him on the way out, and on his way back for the bags. He has to carry them one at a time because they seem to weigh upward of forty pounds each.

"Okay," he says, hefting the second bag, "if you have any questions, please contact our office."

"Thanks." She lowers her chin against her chest as she turns away from the door, mulling everything over.

Peter has enough experience to know that she might not have discussed the assault with anyone except Maggie. He conveys information, knows the limit of his job, but often he ends up a confidant for the victim. And then he feels awkward, a functionary who can never offer what's needed. The overstuffed bag drags against the door jamb, and he nearly stumbles on the landing.

Marina begins to close the door behind him, then hesitates. "Your office is right downtown?"

"That's right. The address is on my card attached to the bail document. Please feel free to stop in, and if I'm not there, someone else will assist you, eight-thirty to four-thirty."

"Actually, I was just wondering if I could catch a ride with you. I'm supposed to meet Mary McConachie in twenty minutes or so."

"Maggie."

"What?"

"Her name's Maggie. But, sure, the police station's about four blocks from our office. I can give you a lift."

"I'll be just a minute, okay?"

"Sure." Peter lugs the bag down the steps and out to the Jeep, then sits with his elbow propped in the open window. Nolin's belongings remind him that he'll soon face moving himself, one way or the other. He really has to call the real estate agent, and if there's been no interest in the house, he'll have to drop the price. Peter sensed impatience in Karen's last email query, which deterred his reply. He takes a perverse satisfaction in this decline into bankruptcy, finds it sort of interesting. Soon there will be no money for cat food and he'll have to ship Anais to California COD.

A young woman appears on the sidewalk in a fern-patterned sundress with a cotton sweater draped over her shoulders, a small woven bag in hand. For a moment he doesn't recognize her. She's almost at the Jeep before he thinks to unlock the passenger door. As she climbs in, he looks the other way, but when he shifts into reverse, he can't miss glimpsing her bare knees and calves.

She sighs. "Thanks. I had to change. I've been holed up in the apartment for four days, moping around, dressed like a slob."

"That's understandable." Peter risks a smile. "Yes, when I met you today my first thought was — this woman's a slob."

For a few seconds Marina doesn't respond, long enough for Peter to fear that he's offended her, crossed the line. Then she smiles at him.

The town is in an afternoon lull, seemingly so peaceful that there will never be another crime. Peter navigates the simple grid of streets. He focuses on his driving, very much aware of the woman beside him.

"Do you like your job?" she asks him suddenly.

"For the most part, yes," he replies, eyes straight ahead.

"Doesn't it get depressing, dealing with this sort of thing all the time?"

"Oh, sometimes, sure. Usually, I'm trying to assist people, even if they don't always understand that, or refuse the offer." He glances at her and is oddly relieved that she's peering out the passenger window. She remains that way, silent, until he pulls into the visitors' parking area in front of the police station.

"Don't get me wrong," Marina says. "I do appreciate your help, and thanks for the ride." She swings her legs out of the Jeep and hesitates before closing the door. "Last night my phone rang three times after midnight. The first time I answered, and after a few seconds, the line went dead. After the third call, I unplugged the phone. The caller's number came back as out of area. But my guess is that it was Todd, with a calling card or something, checking up on me."

Peter frowns. "Listen, you have to tell Maggie about this. She'll pass it on to the investigators, and if it happens again, they might be able to trace the calls another way. Please call me right away if it happens again, and if it's after hours, you've got to call the police. Okay?"

"Yes," Marina says, pausing for a moment on the sidewalk. "It's like a bad dream — last Saturday night and everything since."

"I know, I think, and I'm sorry. But we sure don't want it getting any worse. Don't hesitate to call the police, or the probation office." Peter holds her gaze for a moment until she nods and turns away. He shifts the Jeep into reverse, swears under his breath, and pulls out onto the street.

chapter seven

Since Karen's departure, Peter's dreams have been unusually vivid, unsettling. Not since childhood, as far as he can recall, has his imagination run so rampant at night.

After seven months, he's still not used to the dreams, not in their latest resolution and dimensions. He still spends hours the next day sorting through his subconscious compost, trying to figure out the mystery of images. A rising tide floods a harbour, a city, a valley, then the media network. Variations of vertigo, slipping off the edge of a tiled roof finger by finger, or a parkade tilting away from a nearby explosion. Foreign settings, a village in Iceland or Estonia, recalling films by Andrei Tarkovsky, fires burning, cigarettes smoking in subzero weather. Themes recur, and a few have run often enough around his oblong imagination that, like classic flicks, he can list them by title. Call one of them *Le Cannibal*.

He's hitchhiking somewhere in Eastern Europe, gets a lift in a big yellow Volvo transport driven by a manic androgynous redhead, then is ejected off the chrome passenger running board late one evening, into the soggy fecal ditch below an expressway exit jutting at an angular risk onto a side road, now asphalt but once the trail of successively paler warlords, leading toward a village founded in the Dark Ages.

Walking along the shoulder of a two-lane road, he glimpses fields and pastures bordered by stone walls, farmyards holding primitive equipment, and crude brick houses with thatched roofs. Dogs bark. The autumn sky is overcast, and dusk soon overtakes him. The village isn't in sight yet, so he worries that he misunderstood directions. His pack becomes a burden. He is tired, thirsty, and anxious by the time he reaches the first cross streets and neighbourhood. Then there are shops, civic buildings, a cobbled plaza bordered by several cafés, tables and chairs pushed back under awnings. Lights going out.

He veers to one side of the plaza and comes upon a small café that is still open, though no customers or proprietor are in sight. A bell tinkles as he enters the narrow room. Three small tables line one wall, and along the other is a counter overtop a large display cooler. There, under soft fluorescent light, is an array of varied foodstuffs: salami, proscuitto, various unidentified kaleidoscopic sausages by the slice, cabbage rolls and cabbage salad, meat pies and quiche, and a panoply of glazed tarts, pies, and cakes oozing whipped cream. There are also beverages — bottled water, soft drinks, and two kinds of beer.

Peter rings a hand bell on the counter. After a while, it seems as if he'll never be served, and he's parched and starved. He sets his pack beside one of the tables and rings the bell once more. Then, without waiting, he steps around back of the display cooler, kneels, and slides open the door. He grasps a bottle of water and pours half down his throat. Next he takes a quiche and a pilsner and scuttles to his table. Moments later the beer is gone, and he's holding the crescent remainder of the quiche to his face, mouth full, when from out of a backroom a woman enters the café. She has black hair coiled about her head, olive skin, and expressive dark eyes that target him now, her face creased in a scowl.

Swallowing, Peter lifts his hands. *Pardon moi*, I'll pay. She lets go with a stream of recrimination, out of which he understands only the words *American*, and *police*. No, no, he says, pressing his hands together in apology, eyes imploring. I pay. Do you have a room? Instead of his wallet, he comes up with a leather pouch with drawstring and produces a scarred gold coin that silences the proprietor and puts a glint in her eye.

She leads him through a curtain into the backroom, then up a staircase that overlooks a small courtyard below, open to the night sky above. The woman wears an embroidered top, and a plain black skirt beneath which the shifting of her buttocks becomes more and more alluring the higher they climb. At the very top she opens the door to a cramped room with a six-foot ceiling that forces him to hunch. Peter is so tired and relieved that he smiles. Thank you, *merci*, *danke schön*, he murmurs, collapsing on the bed.

When he awakens later, all is dark. He hears a woman's voice extending the note of an unknown song, an aria. On his knees on the bed, he pushes open the shutters to the single window of his room and peers out. The sky appears as a canopy of purple cloth studded randomly with sequins, and casts only faint light into the well of the courtyard. The air is cool and humid; it must have rained. The brick floor below emits a soft, wet gleam, and a single shallow puddle ripples with drips from the eaves. This image accompanies the woman's voice, words he can't understand in her beautiful tremolo. Gazing downward, he catches the sudden movement of a figure on the stairs, descending. A gloved hand on the railing, the flutter of a cape. For an instant the profile of a face that could be man or woman. Whoever it is leaves by a door on the ground floor, and soon after the song ends ...

chapter eight

Bronco culture, Karen called it the first summer they lived in town, and it got on her nerves pretty much from then on. Toward the end of their relationship it was more often the *fucking* bronco culture, increasingly terse and a bit butch, come to think of it, but with a crude cachet that made him chuckle.

The landscape itself was too arid for Karen. She grew up near the Great Lakes, and this country was too much like desert. Peter was raised in a town that differed by shape and location but where the land, the climate, the values and attitudes were much the same. Only a two-hour stretch of highway between them. So he had umpteen years of conditioning in the redneck sub-ethic.

Sunrise washes over the treed ridges, rock bluffs, and sage-covered foothills. Entering town from the south, the asphalt widens to four lanes, with gas stations, motels, and franchise joints lined along parallel service roads. Log-arch signage lists attractions for tourists. All roads lead by the rodeo arena, with a covered grandstand and a network of corrals situated in a large natural bowl around which the town has grown over the past century. From his second-floor office window Peter can see the pines and junipers at the top of the slope above the exhibition grounds.

No, the town isn't for everyone, by any means. Some professionals are drawn to it for job openings, mostly young and wooed by managers offering moving expenses, but after a year or two many move on. South, back east, or to the United States for more money, or to California for love. That's the case in the probation office where Woodgate's greatest headache is retaining trained staff, something that works a bit in Peter's favour as a trainee in waiting. But headquarters is far away, and it seems to like him right where he sits in front of his computer for auxiliary wages and no promises. Meanwhile the criminology grads come for a while, then move on to more lucrative pastures.

The counter bell peals through the congested air of the office. Everybody hates the thing, since it allows offenders to demand attention as if the probation office were a burger drive-through. But at staff meetings Tammy bemoans what a pain it is picking up the telephone every time the duty officer is required at the front. She would rather listen to the jokers swat the bell.

This morning the bell puts Peter on edge as he makes his way from his desk to the front, and it's no pleasure to see Todd Nolin leaning half over the counter, biceps on display. He's smiling, and Tammy is laughing again at something he's said.

"Here he is," Todd drawls. "Good thing you people get paid by the hour."

Peter ignores the comment and hands a yellow card over the counter. "Complete this, please."

"More paperwork?"

"This is the card you'll fill out from now on when you report. It only takes half a minute. Here's the direction slip for next week, Monday morning. You sign the bottom line." As obnoxious as Nolin is, Peter can believe the man has status around town. He has the large, square features of a bullish athlete raised on lots of red meat. Twenty-four years old and long used to special treatment.

"The bottom line, yeah. That reminds me. There's more stuff I need from the apartment. A friend of mine can pick it all up with his truck tomorrow night after work. Can you let her know?"

"Ah, no. That would mean indirect contact at least between you and Ms. Faro, which is a breach of your undertaking."

"Well, how am I supposed to get my stuff? I want my Uni-Gym and my weights, and I want the TV. That's mine. She can have the little one." As Nolin delivers this information, he places his forearms on the counter and leans shoulders forward to the point that Peter takes a step back.

"Listen, you're not in a position to be making a lot of demands —"

"All I want is the stuff that belongs to me. Stuff she doesn't want, anyway."

"Like the TV?"

"Yeah, like my TV. What's the difference? She hardly watches it. This isn't fair if I can't even collect my own possessions."

"Well, let's think about that. Was it fair to Ms. Faro the night she was hospitalized after your assault?"

"*Alleged* assault! That's what my lawyer says. You can't

even call it assault 'cause there's no evidence."

Peter nods, then takes a breath. "Right."

"So what about my stuff?"

"I'll work on it. Same as before. I'm not approving any acquaintance of yours going over there with a moving van." Now Peter steps forward into Nolin's personal space. "And if the police or myself find that you've breached the conditions of your order, say, by phoning Ms. Faro, for example, you'll be arrested and held in custody."

Nolin's chin is raised, he barely blinks as Peter says this, but he registers something. Then he sneers. "She's telling you that? More likely it's one of her new boyfriends. Ask her about that."

Peter responds by closing the file folder in his hand and turning away from the counter. He's had enough. Nolin's manner provokes an instinct that he dislikes in himself. Finally, the guy saunters out of the office.

Back at his desk, Peter stares out through the smoked glass, raises his eyes beyond the neighbourhood to the steep side hills beyond town dappled with sagebrush. Having roots in a similar town, he guesses he'll never escape the influence it's had in his making. And he won't lose any sleep over that. He knows of former locals who work very hard to deny association with such a town. They live in high-rises in Toronto or Seattle and seem to think they've escaped. He no longer feels that need, and he's always liked the sagebrush. What he doesn't like is resorting to the cowboy stance as if he were squaring off in a bar. It gets his pulse going. He doesn't like the idea that his reason, education, and hard-won maturity, all that stuff, might be swept aside in a moment of plain male fury.

Karen secured a job with the local school board before they arrived, which was the main reason they had come to this crazy town — or city in puberty. But it took several months for Peter to find any employment. She had a decent salary, and he was okay with tending the house, spending an hour or two in the late afternoon preparing new dinners. But that left him about seven hours solo time per day.

So Peter bought a second-hand bike and began exploring the town. During this period, he discovered Amigos, a Mexican-Chinese restaurant with good lunch specials, often chow mein or enchiladas, every day for about four dollars. And he came across the second-hand store, Ivordottor's Used Things, a very long, narrow sort of warehouse. Out front there are often large plywood signs denouncing government taxes and interference, sometimes alluding to another world war. Inside things are stacked into threatening hills of furniture and appliances. Two-by-four shelves sag with cheap china, lamps, and plumbing parts, and the back wall is all books and magazines. Near the front, entirely concealed by junk, the skinny owner has a burrow-like office where he reclines, smoking slim cigars, one eye on a miniature television on his desk linked to a camera aimed at any shoplifters in the many back recesses of the warren.

One afternoon Peter found the Corral Bar, via the short back hallway of the Trailhead Hotel. It's one of the rougher joints he's ever seen. The only unifying feature of the decor is the silver duct tape used to repair the carpet, tables, chairs, and even the mirror behind the bar. There's a hot dog rotisserie, a giant jar of pickled eggs, a beer cooler door that clanks and slams, and a sense of rock-bottom sufficiency about the place. It hosts irregular stripper shows and bands with talent ranging from brutal to not bad.

Something like the town itself, the Corral is enough of a mix and mystery to intrigue Peter. Another thing going for it is that he can sit and sip a draft or two, read a book, and not see anyone from Karen's circle, or the college types. The clientele is mostly Native folks, old-timers, and rednecks. Once he started his current job, though, the jig was up, because the Corral and the probation office have too many customers in common. He hasn't been in there now for a couple of years and sometimes misses the place.

"Peter speaking." He wedges the receiver under his ear and continues pecking away at his keyboard, scanning email from headquarters and deleting almost everything. Not his favourite source of information. "Hello?"

"Peter, it's Sarah Moxey calling. I hope it's all right to phone you at work. I don't want to interrupt anything …"

"Oh, no, that's fine." He stops typing and takes the receiver in hand. For a moment he can't place her name, but he makes no association to any probation file, so it's a welcome little diversion. "Interruptions can be good."

"How have you been doing?"

"Well, I can't complain. Given all the terror and misery in the world, my problems are fairly minor," he says, pleasantly surprised by a social call.

She laughs gently. "Now, now …"

Finally, her face comes to mind — a freckled redhead with a ready smile. She's a speech therapist who worked at the same school as Karen last he knew. Single mom, full-figured. Peter recalls running into her at a gas station two or three months ago, with her daughter riding in the back seat of her Subaru wagon.

"Anyway, I called to see if you'd like to come over for dinner some evening, if you have some time on your hands. It's not easy cooking on your own. I know."

"That's a nice invitation," he says, scrambling for excuses, thinking of their last encounter, her calm interest in him. It was flattering, but … "I do appreciate it."

"We don't have to nail it down, Peter. You can call me, if you like."

"Thanks," he says, grateful for the out.

After a few more pleasantries, she says goodbye. The slight playfulness in Sarah's voice stirs something, and Marina Faro comes to mind — something about her he hasn't quite admitted to himself.

Making arrangements for the accused to obtain his belongings is common in cases of bail for spousal assault. By rights, the police are supposed to handle the matter, but it's never a priority for them. Woodgate's managerial view is that it's better to settle the situation as soon as possible rather than leave any excuse for the guy to go back to the residence. Sometimes it's simplest for the bail supervisor to facilitate the matter, as it seemed in the Nolin/Faro case the other day. But more often than not there's some friend or relative the victim will okay to pick up the stuff. So Peter now considers this as the responsible thing to do. Then he telephones Marina and asks if he can drop by again briefly, mentioning the items on Nolin's wish list. She tells him that later that afternoon will be fine.

The sky is overcast and the air slightly muggy. When he arrives at Arbour Villa, he first sees Fay Kubova, the landlady, in a dress but wearing goggles and orange earmuffs, waging war on weeds with her Whipper Snipper. Then he spots Marina sitting on the lawn with her bare legs outstretched, hair in a braid, leaning her torso and touching her toes with one hand, then the other. Immediately, he feels Mrs. Kubova watching as he studies the young woman, hears her revving her gas-powered weapon. Peter busies himself flattening the back of the Jeep's rear seat to make more space for cargo — Nolin's stupid Uni-Gym and big-screen television.

"Hello again."

"Hi," she says as they meet on the sidewalk and she leads the way to her apartment. Her toned legs and round bottom in running shorts, the glimpse of bare back below her T-shirt, make him self-conscious. She's fairly tall and moves like a gazelle in her runners.

The kitchen is crowded with Nolin's stuff. "That thing's bigger than I expected," he says, examining the workout machine for the best handhold. "I'm not even sure it'll fit in the Jeep."

"Let me help you."

"Oh, no, that's not necessary." Peter lifts one side and half drags it toward the door, stifling a grunt. He catches her eyes rolling slightly before she grasps the other end to help him manoeuvre it out the door and down the steps. Then they lug it over to the Jeep, and it just barely fits. They make a few more trips for the rest of the stuff, piling it in and around the frame of the Uni-Gym. Marina is business-like about it, showing no emotion. She carries a couple of barbell weights, and as she leans over to place them in the Jeep, he glimpses the tail of a blue tattoo on her right hip.

"Well, he was keen on getting the TV, but that'll have to wait," Peter says. He shuts the hatch, wipes his hands, and tries to focus on business himself. Mrs. Kubova is still snipping weeds, but observing everything through her goggles.

"You can pick that up next week," Marina says, a wry glint in her deep brown eyes. "If it's any consolation to him, I sent along his porn tapes."

Peter shifts his gaze from her face toward the Jeep. "Well, I meant he'll have to do without the TV."

She looks down herself, pauses, then asks, "Have you read the police report yet?"

"No, they haven't sent it over yet, but that's not unusual. The police have to finish their paperwork, and it often takes a week or two before we get the details."

"So you haven't read the statement I gave to Maggie and the officer? She asked my consent to release it, said it was important, but that the only people who would see it were the prosecutor and the bail supervisor."

"I'm sure we'll get it soon. But it's not critical to my job at the moment, which is monitoring Mr. Nolin's conditions," he explains, unused to such a query, not certain why she's asking.

"I see." She nods, lightly tossing the loose braid of dark hair. Her manner is serious, safeguarding her thoughts.

Peter plans to deliver this load to the store where Nolin works, leave it on the back step or in the parking lot if necessary, but he's not taking it back to the office. If it causes some embarrassment, well, so what. He drives a measured speed across town and can't help thinking about Marina Faro. He finds her attractive to the point of unsettling. As sometimes happens with women, she seems to intuit her effect upon him and is already on the defensive. He can't recall saying anything the least bit out of line. Her comment about him coming back, and the challenge in her eyes, didn't seem quite fair at first blush. But he can't be sure she even means anything by it. Still, he doesn't like the idea that what he puts into words is outweighed by the language of his body.

chapter nine

Maxine the fax machine, as Peter has named her, is more productive than some office personnel. She relays information free of gossip and opinion, knows her place in the corner, generally does what she's asked, not only faxes back and forth via speed dial, but copies, too, double-sided if you want. She sorts, collates, and staples, all with the touch of her buttons. Sometimes, as a diversion during the day, Peter stands nearby just to pluck the fresh pages from her tray, looking for anything of interest before passing the documents on to Tammy or Janice to be stamped and distributed to the addressee. Often these are offence circumstances written up by the police. They range from strict single-page notes to capitalized cautions or veiled complaints about lifting some drunk off the sidewalk for the umpteenth time, and Peter has become familiar with the standard remarks and spelling errors of certain officers.

So he happens to be standing there as a police cover page scrolls out addressed to him from Maggie McConachie, Victim Services. He starts reading the first page in his left hand while collecting the others with his right and then walks blindly back toward his desk, head down, reading as he goes:

STATEMENT OF:
Marina Theresa Faro
#5–465 Arbour Steet

STATEMENT TAKEN AT:
RCMP Detachment (Interview Room 2)

STATEMENT TAKEN BY:
Cst. K. Bergstrom, w/Ms. M. McConachie, Victim Services

CstB: It is Tuesday at 1530 hours, the twenty-seventh of May. Constable Kevin Bergstrom, with Margaret McConachie, for the purpose of hearing the statement of Ms. Marina Faro. Is this tape picking this up? Yes? I know this has been a very difficult weekend for you, Ms. Faro. Please tell us what your relationship is to Mr. Todd Nolin and then exactly what happened on the twenty-fifth of May, that is, last Saturday night. Take as much time as you need.

MF: Ah, we met about three years ago, I mean, started going out. Before that we had gone to the same high school until he went away to play Junior A hockey. But I didn't really meet Todd until a couple years after graduation, about three years ago. Is this important? I don't know how much to say.

CstB: You're doing fine. Background is helpful, right, Maggie?

MM: Whatever you're comfortable with, Marina.

MF: Well, that was the summer he was drafted … when we started going out. And I really didn't believe he was serious about a relationship, but that was okay. I hadn't had a boyfriend since … high school. Everybody was saying Todd was going to be famous. There were articles in the newspaper. Maybe you remember that? I guess I was flattered or whatever. It was kind of exciting because, well, he was getting all this attention, and it was like he could do no wrong. And he handled it like it was natural. He was only home a few weeks that summer, and when he left, I thought that was that. But he phoned me and kept in touch. He even flew me out to Buffalo twice that winter. The second time I went with his parents, because it was his first game with the Sabres. His dad was so proud.

CstB: Who did they play?

MF: What? [inaudible] Oh, Pittsburgh, I think.

MM: Constable?

CstB: Ah, yes, please go on.

MF: After he signed the first-year contract and all of a sudden had a lot of money, Todd bought a house over in Westridge. It was a couple of streets away from his parents, even a larger house than they have. He rented it out to three of his buddies and stayed there himself when he was home on breaks. The next summer he asked me to move in with him, and I said okay. It's a real nice place with a view of the whole town. He sort of evicted his friends. They weren't too happy. But he had lots of friends then, and they all liked to party at the house. After that season, though, the Sabres delayed renewing the contract or whatever and made no arrangements for him at training camp, or with the farm team. They found some other tough guy they liked better. Todd kept calling his agent and the team office, but they wouldn't tell him anything. It drove him nuts. It was like the whole thing just drifted out of his reach. The agent suggested Todd could maybe play in Europe for a season, or some semi-pro league in the States, but Todd was [inaudible]. Ah, he started drinking every day, buying coke, and wasting money just when it was pretty obvious he had no more coming in. Could I have a glass of that water, please?

MM: Oh, yes … here.

CstB: And when was this?

MF: Thank you. It was, ah, about two years ago that I moved in with him. And it was that fall that things began to change. He wasn't like this when we first got together.

MM: How did he change, Marina?

MF: Um, he had always been so confident, I guess, ever since he was a boy, because he'd always done well at hockey. And he wasn't all that loud-mouthed about it in the beginning, just focused on his training, a bit crazed about it, running and working out all the time. When the team, or the organization, let him go, then he really let go, too. He drank and partied all the time, three or four nights a week, for sure. He started stressing out about every single thing, especially as the money ran out. He'd never had to think about money, but now he needed a job like everybody else. We stayed on in the house way too long. He should have rented it out to cover the payments. I tried to suggest that. But he never really listened to me, and he'd blow up if he thought I was criticizing him.

CstB: What do you mean by "blow up" exactly?

MF: Just lose it, start swearing and slam things around. He'd yell about stuff. I didn't know what he was talking about.

CstB: Did he hit you?

MF: Not in the beginning. He'd say mean things, call me a slut when he had no reason on earth to think that, sometimes grab me by the arm. But he started keeping track of everything I did, asking me where I'd been, who I was talking to on the phone. That's what really got to me. He became jealous, more than jealous, paranoid. I don't know [inaudible]. Plus he was going broke. Last fall he started working at the sports store. Then over the winter he listed the house, with his mother, and luckily it sold within a few months. We moved to the apartment, which was like a reality check. Things were better for a little while.

CstB: The move was to your current address?

MF: Yeah.

MM: How has your relationship been more recently, Marina?

MF: [inaudible] if you call it that, well, pretty weird.

CstB: How so?

MF: He just got so jealous and paranoid over nothing! Every day he needed to know if I had my lunch at work, or met a friend. I mean, he practically even wanted to know what I ate. If we went out, he wouldn't let me out of his sight. So I quit going out on my own with my girlfriends because it wasn't worth fighting every time.

CstB: And he's been physical with you? I mean, prior to last Saturday night?

MF: After I challenged him, months ago, and said I was going to leave. That's when things changed again. That's when he first threatened me. Then he slapped me so hard I nearly passed out. I just never saw that happening to me, but it did, and he said forget about leaving.

CstB: When did this occur?

MF: Oh, I don't know for sure. No, it was February, now that I think about it, because we got into a big fight on Valentine's Day, and I remember thinking, what a sweetheart and how bizarre is this kind of love?

MM: Did he hit you on other occasions, Marina?

MF: Yes [inaudible]. It got to be a habit for him.

CstB: Approximately how often has he assaulted you?

MF: Since February? At least a dozen times.

CstB: But you never called the police?

MF: No, not after he pulled the phone out of the wall the one time I tried.

CstB: And you never thought of leaving him?

MF: What?

MM: Kevin, what line are —

MF: I thought about it all the time! But he said he'd kill me if I left, and I believed him.

CstB: You really think he's capable of that? You feel that threatened? When it comes down to it, very few men carry —

MM: Constable Bergstrom, Kevin, I have to step in here. This isn't a study of some sort. This is Ms. Faro's statement! And let me remind you, she's the victim of a very recent violent assault. Perhaps we should ask the sergeant to sit in and see if he follows your line of reasoning.

CstB: I'm certain he does, Maggie, and you should know where I'm coming from, too. Call him in if you like. [inaudible] Listen, Ms. Faro, some of these questions may seem obvious, or even offend you, and I'm sorry, but we do need this on record.

MF: I understand. Yes, of course, I feel threatened. He's a strong guy. He bench-presses something like three hundred pounds. Maybe you can, too?

CstB: Ah, no, can't say I can lift quite that much. But —

MF: But you get the point? He picked me up by the throat. I couldn't breathe …

MM: [inaudible]. Here's a Kleenex.

CstB: Yes [inaudible]. Well, that brings us to last Saturday night. We need to know exactly what happened.

MF: There were a bunch of guys over to watch the hockey game, then they went out to the bar after. And somebody must have said something about me, that he'd heard a rumour about this party I went to a couple of weeks ago. I don't know if they were razzing Todd or trying to warn him or what. But by the time the club closed, I guess he'd heard enough. He practically kicked down the door when he got home and came right after me, and he's never seemed that crazy before.

CstB: Because of this rumour maybe?

MF: Yeah.

CstB: And what was that?

MM: Is that important?

CstB: Maybe not, Maggie, but when this gets to court it'll come up, and it'll be easier for Ms. Faro to simply confirm this statement rather than go over it all again in a hearing with a lot of people present. Don't you agree?

MM: In part, but —

MF: It's okay. Probably Todd heard I had sex with some guys at a party a couple of weeks ago.

CstB: He wasn't at this party?

MF: No, it was like the first time in six months I was on my own. Todd was away on a buying trip with Dave, the store owner.

CstB: And someone made this story up?

MF: [inaudible]. I'm sure it's exaggerated.

CstB: But you admit there's something to the rumour?

MM: She doesn't have to admit to anything. I just don't see —

MF: Okay, okay, it didn't happen the way they probably said it did, but something happened, yes. Okay? These guys gave me some coke, and we were flirting. And I actually started thinking about Todd, about how crazy my life's been for the past year, like a dog on a leash. But what I did, it was pretty low, I guess. Really thinking that it would, that it would end things with Todd once and for all. But it hasn't [crying].

MM: It's okay, Marina. He isn't interrogating you. This isn't your fault. You haven't hurt anyone or broken any laws.

MF: I've hurt him, haven't I?

MM: You can't blame yourself for that. His violence was a pattern, a cycle you had to get free of, and you don't have to account for yourself or any of it.

MF: I didn't want [crying] …

CstB: We don't need to continue this now.

MM: Marina?

MF: Okay [inaudible].

MM: [inaudible] maybe best. We can finish this another time.

CstB: Yes, that's not a problem. Maybe that's a good idea.

MF: No, no. I meant I want to finish it now, get it over with, please.

CstB: All right, Ms. Faro, I realize you gave us the statement early Sunday morning, which has been written up by an officer. As a result, Mr. Nolin may face several serious criminal charges. Before our report is submitted to the Crown, it's necessary to have your confirmation of that statement. If you do want to conclude this now, is it all right if I review certain portions of your statement, and you can either confirm or comment upon it? Okay?

MF: Yes.

CstB: You said he returned to your residence sometime after midnight and that he was very, ah, agitated when he came in. What was the first thing he said?

MF: He had this weird smile. The first thing he said was: "Hey, little slut. Let's see how much of a slut you can be."

CstB: Did he touch you?

MF: Yes, he came right at me, knocked me onto the couch, and then took hold of my top with his fist. He yanked up, and the shirt tore off me. I tried to kick him. Maybe I did. He lost his balance. And I ran the only way I could, upstairs, even though there was no way out. I thought I could lock myself in the bathroom.

MM: And he came after you?

MF: God, he flew up the stairs. I barely got the door shut before he was pounding on it, screaming about what I wanted, and what I was going to get.

CstB: Pounding on the door?

MF: He hit it three or four times before his fist came through the wood. Then he kicked it in.

CstB: You stated that he then struck you several times?

MF: He grabbed me with one hand by my arm and slapped me with his other hand.

CstB: You then went, or he forced you into the bedroom?

MF: Yes, he dragged me.

CstB: How?

MF: By the back of my bra strap and by my hair.

CstB: You stated that he threw you onto the bed and then straddled you?

MF: Yes, he did.

CstB: He then, ah, he undid his pants and took out his —

MF: Yes.

CstB: [inaudible] the best way to say it?

MM: Say? Oh, Marina, the constable's trying to ask whether Todd was sexually aroused as he did this.

MF: He got that way. He held me down with one hand and stroked himself with the other.

CstB: Okay. And he threatened you at that point?

MF: Over and over, in detail, everything he could think of [inaudible].

CstB: How long after this did the police arrive?

MF: About five minutes maybe.

CstB: You stated that he struck you repeatedly while he held you on the bed?

MF: Yeah [crying].

MM: Constable?

CstB: Uh-huh. That covers it. That's all we need for now, and like I said, Ms. Faro, thank you for this. Hopefully, you won't have to go through it again on the stand. Interview concluded at 1620 hours.

chapter ten

Ever-changing June skies, cloudbursts in the morning, and clear by two o'clock, most days warmer than the one before. Today from his desk Peter watches the last cloud trail away, rubs his hand over his face to wake himself, and notes a trace of stubble along his jaw missed by the razor this morning. Eager for summer, the people below are clad in shorts and T-shirts, and women in cotton dresses brighten up the dusty sidewalks. It's a time he's always enjoyed, this pre-solstice blooming, but this year it does little to lift his spirits.

Karen would be biking every day by now to school and back in her shorts or tights, carrying her teacher's clothes folded into the panniers. He wonders if she'll be teaching in California, or will pursue some new, more lesbian career, perhaps as a feng shui consultant or a welder. More than seven months have passed, a reasonable length of time, an eternity in some respects. But Peter feels as if he's stalled somewhere in

the *cycle of recovery*, by no means *on the rebound* even yet —
the stupid expressions people resort to, that Greg Milchem is
fond of. The language is polluted by little phrases that simplify
experience, cut-rate generic terms for any occasion. No, he
insists on thinking things through a thousand times. Yet it
doesn't ease his missing her.

These days he stares at himself while shaving in the
morning, and sometimes he's daunted just to maintain
himself. He hasn't had a haircut in about five months. Sitting
in a coffee shop, or a diner in the evening when he can't face
cooking alone, he finds himself both intrigued and repelled
by the people around him — all the various faces and scraps
of conversation overheard. He has flashes of despair and
paranoia but puts this down to simply being alone … and
getting used to that.

Often he has a few too many drinks when he ends up at
home. The only conventional pillar of his life was marriage,
but Karen pretty well turned that on its head. There's the
job, which he likes well enough, but it's far from secure. He
doesn't golf or belong to any other secret society. At home
it's just Peter and his bleak imagination, and the television,
until one night in protest he put his foot through it. He's left
it there in the corner of the room so far, the broken screen
jagged and gaping.

His personal situation makes dealing with clients in crisis
both a degree stranger, yet more real, because he feels caught
up in similar chaos. Everything in question. Facing them as
he completes their paperwork and listens to their stories, he
maintains an official reserve, and they might assume that his
own life is as ordered as can be.

At lunchtime he walks to Frieda's Deli and orders schinkenbeck on rye, but by the time he gets through the counter lineup and turns to find a seat, he's claustrophobic, so he takes his sandwich outside. Along the sidewalk he notes the signs and displays of the small-town stores. People often angle their way across the street through slow-moving traffic. He recognizes too many, not all by name, and he dislikes the idea that his face is also familiar in this way. Peter recalls the heady freedom he felt travelling, being in Lisbon or Prague for the first time alone and anonymous, the allure and sophistication of foreign cities. Here, in this town, two pickups halt mid-block as buddies push back their caps and chat through open windows, traffic be damned, their dogs in back staring at passersby and barking when Peter eyes them back.

A leggy woman in a sundress catches his attention, a teller from the bank that will soon foreclose on his house. She even smiles briefly before turning into the drugstore. That's enough to unsettle Peter, provoke his desire, which lately paces in his brain like a captured bull muskox. He can't recall having more than a brief conversation with a woman in the past seven months, never mind asking someone to meet for coffee or badminton or whatever people do now to get together. Having been secure in a relationship for a long time, somehow the idea of seeking companionship seems ridiculous or humiliating. Not that he revels in bachelorhood, as some men pretend.

As for the invitation to dinner from Sarah Moxey, thanks but no thanks. Sarah's quite attractive, thirty something, with bushy red hair and a big smile. She's probably quite intelligent, too, and sensitive, athletic, creative. And for all those reasons he tells himself to steer clear.

Greg Milchem, the psycho-babbling probation officer in the next cubicle, can go through a relationship quicker than a box of Cheerios. Peter sometimes overhears him whispering to his new loves on the phone. Everyone in the office is used to Greg's cycle of infatuation — moving in, future plans with the new woman, then trouble such as she's allergic to cats and he has three Siamese, or she doesn't golf, which leads to the breaking point, moving out, then half a week's despondency and maybe a mental health day.

Some people ricochet through life from one relationship to the next. Peter is amazed at their enthusiasm and faith that the next one is the real thing. Being single, he now finds himself tense around some women, those who carry an aura of expectation. Everything in question. Karen no longer preoccupies his thoughts as she did in the first few months after she left. For a while, apart from dire financial worries and occasional thoughts of suicide, he almost had his mind to himself.

Now he finds himself thinking of someone else, wondering how she's doing, what she's doing at any given moment. Even this feels wrong, as if he's breaking some rule with his mind. It's well within the lines of duty to call her again, but each day Peter gives it too much thought and ends up putting it off.

chapter eleven

Marina Faro works for Hartland Insurance as an assistant to one of the local corporate agents. Among her duties is delivering documents back and forth around town in a gold Camry banded with office advertising. She sits tall and serious behind the wheel, with her long dark hair combed back, often sunglasses, a bit of executive style. Her boss knows she looks good on the job, which doesn't hurt business. He was understanding enough to give her a few days off last month without asking many questions and was glad to have her back.

Peter spotted Marina driving that car over a year ago but didn't recognize her when they met face to face. He did the first time he saw Marina driving again. His eyes followed her past, going through an intersection on a yellow light, and then somebody was honking behind him — green means go. In recent weeks he's seen her several times, his attention alert to the gold Camry now.

"Peter Ellis speaking …" He's sitting at his desk, doing a form by rote, filling in the blanks.

"Hi, it's Marina Faro. You left a message … yesterday?"

"Yes, ah …" He lays his pen flat and pushes forward in his chair. "Thanks for getting back to me. I don't mean to bother you. It's just a routine check-in."

"Okay."

"In order to monitor bail conditions, in this case regarding Mr. Nolin, it's helpful to have periodic contact with any person named on the order, such as yourself."

"I see."

Behind her voice he can hear subdued office noise. Once again he feels the strange effect of her voice, which is a bit deeper and more mature than her years. How old is she? Maybe twenty-five?

"So I just wanted to check if you have any concerns. Mr. Nolin is prohibited from any contact with you, so is he abiding by that condition?"

"I guess so. He hasn't come by, or called, if that's what you mean."

"Yes, well, that's good," he says hastily, ready to hang up and settle his nerves.

"But last week flowers were delivered to me at work. There was no card. I think they must have been from Todd."

"Really." Peter grabs a pen to jot notes in the file. "I don't mean to seem intrusive, but that's exactly the sort of thing it's good for us to know about. I mean, it's not unusual that a man will do something like this out of remorse. But it's not always a good sign, I'm afraid, and —"

"Todd doesn't know the meaning of remorse. The flowers came on Friday. I thought of calling, but didn't get around to it."

"Of course." He taps the pen on the ruled paper. "What I'm going to do is advise my boss, because this is a breach of his bail."

"So he can be arrested?"

"Perhaps. Certainly if there's evidence he sent the flowers. But you say there was no indication of who they came from?"

"No, and they were delivered when I was out."

"From which florist?"

"I don't know. I could check with the secretary. She might remember."

"It could be very helpful to know. Would you mind asking her? What I'll do is run it by my boss. Can I call you back there?" He's on his feet, the file in hand.

"Sure."

Peter makes a beeline for Woodgate's office where the manager is pecking out email with two simian index fingers as he does for hours every day. "Excuse me, George?"

Woodgate raises his big right hand to the door. One of his more irritating habits is to keep his staff waiting while he finishes his thought, which can take a while. But Peter has made the mistake of speaking too soon, and he can't afford any more wrath.

"What is it, Alice?" Woodgate asks finally, lifting his chin.

"It's about the Nolin file. I just got off the phone —"

"Todd Nolin, yes. Good hockey player. Shame he didn't stick it out in the big league."

"Yes, apparently. Now he's on bail for spousal assault. And I was just talking to the victim, Marina Faro. She says that flowers were delivered to her office last week. She thinks it was him."

Woodgate nods. "Probably."

"A clear breach of his order. So I'll do up an RCC?"

"Ask for a warrant?"

"Yes, I think so."

Woodgate smiles, shakes his head, and turns back to the computer. "*I* don't think so."

"What? Pardon me. I'm not sure I take your meaning."

"Yeah, okay, it's a breach of his order, Alice. And it's impossible to prove. So your report to the Crown would be a waste of time."

"I think we know which florist the flowers came from. Ms. Faro is checking with her office secretary."

Woodgate sighs heavily. "Jesus, and you picture the police headed to the flower shop with the siren on? Trying to trace a bill that was paid for in cash by some fucking pal of Nolin's, and then all these people being dragged into court before Judge Vanderkraan? For a bouquet of carnations?"

"I'm not sure what kind of flowers they were. I can check."

"For Christ's sake!" Woodgate's great hairy arm reaches out and slams the office door.

Marina accepts his explanation about the flowers over the phone, but he feels like a desk-bound bureaucrat speaking the absurd. He recalls their semantics in her apartment. *Prevent* versus *prohibit*, a judicial verb, photocopied over and over for all concerned, meaning diddly-squat.

He next encounters Marina at the post office. That is, he's walking past on a Wednesday afternoon and sees her at the end of the lineup with a bundle of office mail in her arms. Stamps, surely, he needs stamps. For a moment he stands behind her, the dark chocolate hair swept over one shoulder revealing the nape of olive skin. Then she turns.

"Oh, hello," he says cautiously because it's not uncommon for those he meets in the course of work to pretend they don't recognize him on the street. The bail supervisor reminds them of what they want to forget.

"Hi," she says with a level gaze that gives away nothing.

"Busy day?" He glances at the stack of envelopes she's holding.

"The usual. And for you?"

"Just out to grab a coffee."

"I don't think they sell coffee here."

He smiles; she's quick. "I need a packet of stamps."

"I see." She moves forward with the line. He follows, but not too close. Everyone else in the post office looks second-hand around her. And they are either distracted or half-asleep.

Peter leans toward her slightly, and in a low tone asks, "This isn't the place to discuss much, of course, but has anything else happened? I felt like I wasn't much help the other day. But I hope it won't stop you from calling again. I mean, if there's anything you need to talk about."

"Nothing urgent."

He nods, but detects what?

"Did you ever read that report from Maggie?" she asks.

"The interview transcript? Yes, well, I went over it quickly." This amounts to a white lie, but one meant to save her further discomfort. He'd read the report with care.

Her brows rise ever so slightly before she shifts her gaze to the next available postal clerk. Quietly, she says, "I had to read it over before I signed the statement. And it's awful, spelling it all out like that. You must think I'm a bitch, or worse."

Peter glances around, drops his voice to a whisper. "No, I don't. It's my job. And this may be no comfort to you, but your situation isn't so unusual. My opinion doesn't make any difference, but just so you know, if anything, I respect you more for getting out. A lot of people never do."

"I can help you over here," the postal clerk pipes up.

"That's nice of you to say," Marina says to Peter as she turns toward the wicket. "You know, I hardly ever buy stamps for myself. Who writes letters anymore?"

Point taken, he thinks, with no idea how much she meant by that.

Every morning he's always rushing to get to work on time. Apart from beer, liquor, and lately cigarettes, he lays in a good stock of juices and vitamin tablets, as well as frozen dinners, mini-wheat cereal, lettuce, pasta, and the odd steak. Mornings, he takes Tylenol with his grapefruit juice, unrolls the window driving, squints into the sunrise, and drinks in the cool air.

For ten minutes he drives through the woods, over rangeland speckled with cattle, before dipping into the depression of the town. Sagebrush skitters across the four black lanes, bunching along the low-side concrete wall. Passing the mall, he spies Levi Charlie and a couple of pals staggering through the empty parking lot, heading for the rodeo grounds and their daytime beds in the fringe grass. Sleep well, friend, perchance to dream.

By Friday afternoon, Peter is tired of crime and its grey fallout. He sits at his desk, scanning the office circulars, reviewing emails from management, making a few calls. In between, from behind the smoked glass, he watches the street below. It's Friday afternoon in California, too. Yeah, Friday evening in Montreal, midnight in Prague, and tomorrow morning in Japan.

The phone rings in the next cubicle, and he can't help overhearing Greg Milchem cooing and giggling about the picnic plans he's lined up with his latest flame. The guy hangs up and releases a great sigh. "Ah, life is good."

"What's that?" Peter asks, leaning back in his chair.

"Do you ever have those moments when your life feels like a perfect tee shot, sailing out there and you can't wait to follow the ball?"

"No … maybe because I don't golf."

"Well, we all have our ups and downs, Peter. But you should try it sometime. It's a nice way to spend an afternoon." Milchem twirls out of his chair, picks up his little turquoise nylon lunch sack and his jacket, and winks. "It just happens that this evening I have a better offer. See you Monday!"

Peter starts packing up himself, in no great hurry, but ready to go. It's twenty after four and he's tying his shoe when the phone rings.

"It's Marina Faro?" she says as though he might not remember.

"Yes," he replies, tightening his laces and planting his feet, "how can I help you?"

"Last week in the post office you said I could call if anything came up."

"Of course." He checks his watch and notes Woodgate leaving his office, headed for the back door. Everyone waits about five seconds before filing out the door behind him, leaving Peter alone.

"It's about the TV."

"Yes, the giant screen. I remember. Todd's mentioned it a couple of times when reporting in. I guess he'd like to have it. But you don't have to worry about that, not for now."

"I guess not anymore, because it's gone."

"What?" She's caught his interest. He hauls open the drawer of his cabinet and fishes out the Nolin file, his fingers confused. "Since when?"

"I just got home from work. It spooked me when I walked into the living room and saw the TV gone."

"Marina," Peter asks, grabbing a handful of hair, "are you alone? Have you been through the apartment? Listen, get outside, now. Go to the manager's —"

"It's okay. I've been upstairs. It was stupid maybe. But there's no one here."

"Okay, okay ..." He taps his pen on the ruled lines of the open file. "Did you call the police? I'll call them. Do you feel safe there? Is there anywhere else you could stay? No, I can understand that. Yes, they'll have it on record. They'll keep an eye out on their patrols. Our office is closed now until Monday. You shouldn't hesitate to call the police. That's what they're there for. I'm off now. That's right. Yeah. Oh, I believe you. Sure, it's gone. I'm a bail supervisor, not a cop. No, no, I don't mind. I mean, it is after hours. But no one's going to interrogate you. The point is that he's *prohibited* from any contact with you, and from being anywhere near your place. Plain and simple. I hear you, yes. Ah, I suppose not. It's not really out of my way. No, that's fine. I'll stop by in a few minutes."

At the back door of the office Peter briefly considers taking one of the office Jeeps. But if he does, then he'll have to bring it back in half an hour and will end up logging more overtime for which auxiliary staff aren't paid. He thought he made it clear to her that his workday was over. Nothing says he has to go look at a missing television. It's a matter for the police. But he extended the offer, and she called. Strictly speaking, it's after hours, but he's not feeling too strict about much these days. And he certainly isn't pressed for time. His house won't be any emptier if he's late getting home.

The afternoon heat is easing with a breeze. Peter climbs into his rusty Bronco, hesitates another moment behind the wheel, then turns the key. The traffic is a bit crazy — big shiny pickups roar down the main drag, billowing diesel smoke. Hell, these guys don't dawdle around. What's wrong with him?

Fay Kubova is out front watering the flower beds in front of Arbour Villa. The old woman's head turns as Peter parks in the lot, then her eyes follow him along the sidewalk. He hasn't got a file this time, and his empty hands make him feel conspicuous.

"Your marigolds are doing very well, Mrs. Kubova," he says with an approving glance that doesn't fool her.

She lifts her chin and squints. "Yes, they are. Who are you — some kind of flower inspector?"

Peter smiles. "No, no."

The old manager scowls. She has a two-foot brass wand that sprays a perfect cone of water — always some kind of potential weapon in her hands.

"I'm just here to speak to Ms. Faro for a moment."

Mrs. Kubova shakes her head, takes hold of the green hose, and hauls it across the lawn. He's already on edge, and her manner has a way of making him feel downright paranoid.

Peter climbs the four steps in front of unit 5 and knocks on the door.

"Hi," Marina says, moving back as he enters. She changed out of the skirt she wore to work and shed her jacket, kept the white blouse, wearing loose khakis and bare feet beneath. Her toenails are painted an azure blue.

"Ah … hello." He pauses, gestures outside, tongue-tied again. She arches a fine eyebrow. "It just occurred to me that your landlady might have seen who took the T.V."

"Nope, I already asked her. She said she was downtown for about an hour, like she is almost every day. That's when they must have taken it. Her husband wouldn't notice."

"So they either lucked out or waited until she left?"

"Todd would know she's usually not here after lunch." Marina's chin is tipped toward her chest, her dark hair swept to one shoulder as she paces the room.

"Well, we have to call it in to the police. This is a serious breach. He obviously doesn't care about the court order, and that's meant to protect your safety."

"The piece of paper you left me last time?"

"Yes, the undertaking to a judge, I mean. It's a further offence if he's not keeping those conditions."

She shakes her head, her cheeks flushing. "You don't know Todd. If he gets pissed off, he doesn't care about anybody's rules. That's why he didn't stay long in the NHL. He was always taking stupid penalties for nothing, and he cracked some guy's skull with his stick about the third game he played. That piece of paper of yours just provokes him. Trust me."

As serious as the matter is, Peter finds it hard to concentrate fully on what she's saying, due to her face, the butterfly lips, her whole stunning self. She's clearly bright and capable. He turns away and stares out the window. Despite all the spousal cases he's worked on, all the research and statistics, the question flashes through his mind: *Why did she live with an ape like Nolin, especially after he started slapping her around?* It's a question better left alone for fear of the answer. And now that bastard walks right into her apartment in broad daylight.

"You're right. I don't know Todd. I don't understand all that's going on here. But I don't care if he's Wayne Gretzky. He either lives by those conditions or he'll be arrested." Peter meets her eyes for a moment, then glances away.

"He's not stupid," she says.

"No one said he was."

"I mean, he's smart enough not to give himself away. I doubt he actually came here today. It would have been one of his friends."

"Your door was locked? He must have given someone the key. Even so, he should be charged with breaking and entering on top of the breach."

"You seem to put a lot of faith in the rule book. Not everyone cares that much." She watches him until he turns to answer her.

"That's beside the point. It doesn't really matter what I think. There's a court order in place."

"What about the flowers?"

Peter clenches his teeth. "Like I said before, they couldn't have proved the connection in court, apparently, but it's documented in the file."

"And they won't prove this!" she cries, pointing at the imprint on the carpet where the giant television once sat, letting her hand fall against the top of her thigh. Her gesture focuses his eyes on the khaki cloth that's temptingly snug just below her waistband. "What it proves is that he can do whatever he damn well wants and get away with it."

The absence of the television unbalances the living space, with a blue leather couch positioned for viewing. The rest of the room is Spartan — a recliner that matches the couch, one other chair, a stereo system in a glass cabinet, and a few mostly bare shelves.

Much later, years after the story ends, he might forgive himself if he remembers solely how she looked at this moment. Her white blouse and khakis complement the rich tone of her skin and her slim frame. Dark chocolate hair frames her angry face with a beauty that blurs his focus. With each passing moment he finds himself succumbing further to the tow of her tide, like the sea creature tattooed on her skin, or as if she herself is a porpoise he might save from a seine net.

"You think he's capable of carrying out his threats?" Peter asks.

She turns away two paces, hands on hips, shoulders rising and falling with deep breaths. "Yeah, I know he'll try."

Her words penetrate him like needles of ice. He speaks more gently. "I know the process and the documents and all that might not give you much security. But that's the extent of my job — I keep a file. I'm not a cop. You have to call the police again. Maybe you could stay with a friend tonight or over the weekend?"

Despite the sense of threat, in contrast to it, the evening light through the windows is pleasant, and the green coin leaves of aspens flip gently in the June breeze. She places her hands over her face for a moment, then runs her fingers through her hair and turns.

"You know, you said it doesn't matter what you think," she says as her blue toes step toward him. "Actually, it does matter now to me. Even if it shouldn't."

Without thinking he takes her offered hand and ends up holding it for a moment too long.

chapter twelve

Marina lifts her open hand, and he takes it in his own — as simple as that. Neither lets go, and she looks up at him, offering her eyes. Gems. For a few seconds he tries to guess what might come of this either way, then attempts to reason with himself: *This is crazy. Stop it!* He shifts his attention to the watch on his wrist. The workday's done, and he's out here in no man's land like any other rootless human. Friday evening. They've already talked about the missing television, about all that's necessary. Her white blouse is untucked; only the middle three ivory buttons are fastened.

"I should go," he says.

She nods, their fingers still linked. "You should, I guess, but you don't have to. You don't have a court order to live by."

He laughs, gently releasing her hand. "Not exactly."

"You won't be arrested for being here, will you?"

He sees a trace of a real smile for the very first time. "No, I'd just lose my job. I mean, if they knew I was here for anything other than business, which is why I came. Not to offend you, I hope. Believe me —"

"None taken."

She smiles fully now, and Peter feels it in his chest, the falter of his breathing.

"You like your job," Marina says. "You told me that already."

"Well, for the time being. It's the only semi-stable thing in my life these days, and not even all that secure when it comes down to it." He turns toward the door, then gazes out the window across the broad lawn to where Mrs. Kubova is bent over on a search-and-destroy dandelion mission with her trowel.

"How so?" Marina has seated herself at one end of the blue leather couch crossways, her feet drawn up, toes like little shells.

Peter tells her the basic circumstances of his job, the fact that he's been doing it for almost two years but hasn't been trained, and that he works as an auxiliary. He does this while looking out the window.

"I don't mean to be nosy, but what about the rest of your life?" she asks. "Things aren't going so well?"

"Oh, I'm fine," he says quickly, but then makes the mistake of meeting her eyes. She moves her feet a bit closer to her bottom, her hand touching the couch in front of her. Then she wraps her arms around her knees. "I mean, my wife left me about seven months ago now. That was a bit rough. Now she doesn't want to pay out on the mortgage anymore and the house isn't selling, but I guess bankruptcy isn't the end of the world." He smiles.

She smiles in return. Peter takes two steps and sits as though the couch is one big curved leather magnet and his body is caught in its pull. He elaborates on Karen's departure, how it took him by surprise. Marina is attentive. With simple questions she elicits more than he can imagine telling anyone, let alone this young woman. She's younger than he is by ten years or so, and to his own ears he sounds much too middle-aged. Peter is flattered by her interest, drawn in by the depth of her eyes and the olive cleavage showing from her white blouse. He runs his fingers through his hair again and again, scratches his neck, pinches his shoulder, thinking: *Wake up now!*

Finally, his words trail off into a few minutes of silence, and then hers begin. She pushes back her hair with her fingers, explains that she was raised by her mom, that her parents were divorced when she was twelve. After that she and her mom moved here where Marina began high school.

"I hated it at first. I didn't know a single person, but by grade ten or so I guess I'd fit in, made some good friends." She looks away from him, out the window. "This time of year always reminds me of Larry, the first boy I went out with."

At this shift in the conversation Peter feels every bit his age, since he can barely remember high school. He has another spell of nerves and again tells himself to get the hell out. But he does wonder why she's bringing all this up, why the need to tell him about this part of her life. So he lays his head back against the blue leather and listens, which seems to be all she wants.

"Larry wasn't a well-known guy. None of my friends really knew him. He was kind of shy. Not the party type. We met in a class, history or math, one of those. He did really well in school and played on the basketball team. Pretty cool in a quiet way. For our first date he asked me out for coffee! I mean, I didn't drink much coffee at seventeen, so it was funny, and we laughed about it later. He lived on a ranch and started drinking coffee when he was ten or something, like his dad.

"They didn't own the ranch, which was huge and belonged to some guy from Germany who came over once a year. Larry's dad had owned a place but lost it in a market slump. His dad was a nice guy and talked to me quite a bit the times I visited them. Not your typical rancher type, but that's what he was. He loved that life and had managed this big ranch for years, making a pretty good living. And Larry's mom worked at the library in town. After we started going out, he'd pick up her car there after school, this giant old blue Chevy with bench seats …"

"Like an Impala or Caprice?" he prompts, wanting her to continue.

"I guess. All I remember for sure was the bench seats, front and back." She laughs, coy or nervous, perhaps a bit of both. "So, yeah, Larry Thompson was my first boyfriend. We went out for the last part of grade twelve. I spent time at his place, out at the ranch with horses. He was so good with them. That's when his real confidence came out — with the horses. His parents were just great, and being there was like a home I'd never had.

"So in June we were going to graduate, and we had finals to study for. Both of us planned to go to college. Well, I studied. It didn't seem like Larry had to. But there were a lot of parties going on by then, and one Friday night, four of us got together, my friend Shelley and a boy she was dating who Larry knew. I drove the car because Larry had already had quite a bit to drink, which was unusual. Somebody told us about a party at The Ashtray, which is out of town up this rough dirt road. And I remember the car scraping bottom and thinking I didn't want to face Larry's mom if I damaged her car …" Marina raises a hand to her mouth, memory clouding her eyes.

Peter knows that this is more than nostalgia for her. He can recall those teenage parties himself, launched with bonfires in some gravel pit or field well outside of town, since they were too young to drink but hell-bent on doing so. Old cars and pickups gathering, plowing through the dust they raised, parked haphazardly among the wild grass and weeds. Woodsmoke and pot in the air, young faces circling through the firelight, a splash of beer on a girl's T-shirt.

The site she mentioned, the Ashtray, is a local landmark — a three-hundred-foot cliff with an alluvial pile of gravel and stone at its base. Old windows, tires, and bikes, even a vehicle from years before now half buried by the rest, have accumulated there. It's some sort of thrill for rednecks to see the fall, hear the glass shatter, the metal snapping over the rocks below. "What happened, Marina?" he asks gently.

She clutches her knees, face concealed. Then she lifts her head, sighs a blue breath, and shifts her feet to the floor. Wiping her eyes, she stands and walks toward the window. "I remember there were so many people gathered around the fire and their cars, a lot of noise. This was June, but it wasn't that warm, kind of cool, the grass damp. Larry and I took a walk away from the crowd for a while. We were completely in love and really didn't have a clue, you know? School was ending, and we couldn't imagine being apart. Maybe that's why he was in a crazy mood, drinking quite a bit, smoking some pot.

"We went back toward the party. Shelley and her boyfriend were sitting with others on the tailgate of a pickup. And I don't know if anybody said anything, I didn't hear it, but afterward someone said they heard this other guy say something to

Larry about the edge. Something like a dare. Anyway, Larry started walking toward the cliff. He was wearing this cowboy shirt, the kind with a yoke over the shoulders, and I can still see the red yoke on his shirt as he moved away from me."

Marina's arms are folded across her chest as she gazes out the window. "There was fog in the gorge, like the suds of a bubble bath in a giant tub. I remember thinking it was almost level with the ground and I was sober, but I couldn't tell exactly where the edge was. I recall having those thoughts all in an instant, in that order, and I opened my mouth, but my voice was frozen." She opens her arms. "At the last moment he raised one arm suddenly as if to catch his balance, then he was gone ..."

"Jesus, Marina, I'm sorry," Peter whispers.

After a while, she nods, then turns her tear-stained face toward him. "So when you talk about being taken by surprise, someone leaving your life, I know what you mean."

When Peter next dares to look at his watch, he sees that almost two hours have passed. Her ankles now rest on his thighs, and he's holding her feet, caressing her blue shell toes. They've talked the entire time; the physical touch came with her trust. At first she placed one foot against his thigh, and it startled him, like a hot wire. Later she stretched her leg and then placed both feet in his lap. After a few minutes, he took them in his hands. When he studied her feet more closely, he received another jolt, which he realized she had been waiting for. Between her smaller toes there was skin, tiny webs that made her feet seem a bit like those of a water creature. Marina waited for his reaction, and he tried to control it, so she wouldn't be offended in any way. She smiled. They talked a while longer, and her toes weren't mentioned, which he appreciated, whether she did or not.

Not suddenly, but very certainly, it strikes him that he has to leave. *She's too beautiful.*

At the door she kisses him quickly, then holds his wrists to his sides as he leans toward her mischievous lips. "Maybe next time, if I see you?"

"Marina, I'd like that, if it were any way possible. But this is —"

"That's two *ifs* and a *but*." She opens the door. "I guess we'll see?"

"Yes," he says, taking her hand briefly again. Her telephone on the counter catches his eye. "I can't call here, you realize? I mean, about anything other than business. Your phone is monitored."

She nods. "We'll see."

Although it's after seven, it's daylight still in mid-June, the heat drifting into the evening. Peter scans the parking lot and the street as he pulls out but sees no one paying notice. It's Friday evening, and kids are cruising around in their jalopies and 4x4s. An engine revving behind him at a traffic light unnerves him. In the rearview mirror is a trio of laughing teenagers. Only when he drives through town and is a good piece down the highway does his breathing settle.

chapter thirteen

Peter spends many disjointed hours over the weekend gathering the last of the things Karen left behind. He sorts them into boxes to either mail COD to California or drop off at the Salvation Army. While handling her ski clothes, he chokes up for a moment. Then he stuffs down the sweaters, knickers, and memories and tapes the box eight times over.

The house has been for sale for months now, with no interest at all. The market is flat due to the recession and local unemployment, the realtor says, but tells him he should cut the lawn. By this point, Peter will consider even the lowest of lowball offers, because it's either that or repossession in the near future. Sitting on the back step with his first beer at about eleven o'clock on Sunday morning, unshaven, shades on, Peter rather likes the unkempt lot, the way the yard has gone to dandelion and thistle seed. But he has noticed that the neighbours no longer speak to him and that the realtor has a point. So he finds a scratch pad and begins a list of things he has to do or obtain: get mower fixed, weed killer, Comet, bathroom, Windex, windows, bottles, papers, recycling.

In other words, he tries to keep busy, to keep his mind and imagination on track, yet Marina keeps whirling through his thoughts. Here he is a half-year or so barely free of Karen's hold on his mind only to find himself mooning around like a teenager. A part of him resents that. Another part seems hard-wired to need a woman's company. She's utterly beautiful the more he thinks about it. But this thing with Marina Faro is lunacy.

On Sunday evening Peter phones his parents for the first time in months. After Karen's departure, his mother checked in every week until he let it be known he had nothing to say, no explanations, and needed time to himself. This Sunday night, though, he needs some reminder of who he is.

A few years ago his parents retired to a modest beach house on the Sunshine Coast, a half-acre lot on the rocky waterfront. His father constructed a dock meant to withstand any future tsunami and protect the thirty-six-foot wooden launch he's restoring. When Peter calls, his father answers the phone and brings Peter up-to-date on the project. Then his mother comes on the line, so openly pleased by the call that for a moment he can't speak. This, too, she understands. Although he skirts the details of ruin and despair, she knows what he needs. Her voice is enough as she tells him the latest news about his two successful sisters who, she says, always ask after him.

That night he dreams he's on his father's boat, bound for California, and is swept overboard by a wave. The white launch is swallowed by darkness, with no land in sight. On the crest of a wave a sleek brown creature appears. He takes it for an otter or a seal. But its head turns, and the profile is that of a woman, long hair like a fine cape over her neck and shoulders. She beckons him, gracefully suspended in the water, until he dog-paddles to her side. Then she circles him in the water, bids him to take hold, and rolls under. Her lower body is as smooth and muscular as a porpoise's. His hands grasp her tail, and he's pulled under. Down, down, through inky depths. The mermaid is at home in this environment, but Peter's terror grows with the pressure of each yard they plunge until he has to let go. But instead of rising back to the surface he keeps sinking, only slower, and alone ...

Peter snaps awake, gasping, at five-thirty in the morning and can't get back to sleep. So he gets up, makes coffee, and sits at the table across from a pile of unopened, unpaid bills. Even their curt final notices are boring by this point. Cable service was cut off last week and the phone will be next, but he couldn't care less. Inevitably, sitting there in his shorts and T-shirt with his coffee and the rising sun, he reviews the events of the past year or so and actually considers having a drink, but settles for a cigarette and shrugs it off. He also contemplates packing the Bronco with his essentials and just driving away, but where to? For now he heads to the bathroom to shave and shower.

The morning is especially bright, not a cloud in the sky, and the rangeland and the lake teem with colour. He rounds the last bend before the city limits and comes upon a motorhome in flames, slowly pitching off the opposite bank as the brake cables melt and inky vinyl and rubber smoke billows up the sagebrush slope. There are police cruisers angled across the highway, lights flashing, one lane of traffic. Just as Peter arrives, so does the pumper truck from town, with firefighters in bright blue jumpsuits scrambling to their tasks.

He shifts the Bronco into low gear and joins the inbound queue without having to stop. An elderly couple stands holding on to each other well behind the police car. One officer is on the radio, while another directs traffic. He recognizes Constable Bergstrom with the wand and lifts his hand as he passes, his forehead suddenly prickling with sweat.

Peter is the first to arrive at the office, which hasn't happened for at least six months. When he turns on the main lights, the computers hum after their midnight screening from headquarters. The rooms and chairs are empty, but an hour from now they'll be buzzing. From time to time over the past thirty-odd years, Peter has had the peculiar sense of being an imposter in his own life, but he's never suffered it quite so intensely as at this moment. Does everyone have a little imposter or a bit of the criminal in them? Everything about the office space seems alien to him now, yet he'd miss it if he had to leave.

"Pete!"

He jumps, then rubs his back as if it's just a twinge. Tammy barges into the staff room, throws a sweater onto the chair she favours, and opens the fridge to stow her Tupperware lunch. "No coffee? First one in puts the coffee on, remember?"

"Right, good morning," he mumbles, fumbling through the process.

Within ten minutes the room feels crowded with arrivals. The greetings taste stale. Greg Milchem launches right into the latest sound bite of his latest romance. Tammy is all ears. Peter hastens away to his cubicle, sprinkling the carpet with his coffee.

He starts reading through the stack of backlogged office circulars, a list of emails. Then he wanders out to collect the newest files and materials from the mail slots at the front of the office. At about nine-thirty the first intakes shuffle in, ripe from having spent a night or two in jail. He's tied up for almost two hours. As soon as he gets back to his desk for a breather, the call comes.

"Alice?"

Tammy smirks as he passes by her desk. Peter stands in the doorway while Woodgate completes an email without turning his head.

"Yes," the manager then declares, reaching for a paper on the side of his desk, "you seem to have a special interest in the Nolin file."

How did Woodgate find out so fast? Peter wonders. Someone must have noticed his Bronco parked at Arbour Villa after hours — a cop on a drive-by check perhaps, old Mrs. Kubova next door maybe, or even Nolin himself or some acquaintance. Whoever it is wasted no time passing on the information.

"Alice?"

"Yes, pardon me," Peter says, taking a deep breath. "Listen, George, I'm sure you don't want excuses …"

"Excuses? No, I don't. Have we had some sudden upsurge in bail cases or something else unknown to me? Is there any good reason you can't do the report?"

"Report?"

"I just asked you if you'd take on the Nolin PSR. Are you feeling okay? Your hearing seems impaired."

"No, I mean, yes. I'm fine! I can do the report, of course, you bet. I didn't expect that case would come to trial for some time."

"It didn't. That boy must have found a good lawyer, because they cut him a deal. But who knows the circumstances? I suppose that's why they asked for the report."

"Yes, I'll get it started this week … tomorrow."

"Good." Woodgate stares at Peter as the younger man backs out of the office, then bumps into the secretary's desk, grinning nervously.

"Watch where you're going, Pete!" the secretary cries.

chapter fourteen

"Cut a damn deal, I guess," Peter whispers under his breath after he has a chance to review the pre-sentence report request for Todd Nolin. There were five original charges: assault causing bodily harm, sexual assault, unlawful confinement, possession of a restricted weapon, and resisting a police officer. If convicted of all these, an offender could expect at least two years in jail, possibly more, meaning federal time. Somehow they've been reduced and amended to two: assault, what is called common assault, and unlawful storage of a firearm. The defence lawyer's name is unfamiliar to Peter, which means an out-of-town, expensive suit. Apparently, the prosecution has agreed to a joint submission on sentencing, one that doesn't seek jail, but a conditional sentence served in the community, with the opportunity to attend spousal assault and anger-management counselling. Legally, it's considered a custodial sentence, but if Nolin can abide by the conditions, he won't see the inside of a cell.

Peter sighs and shakes his head. He met Marina Faro within three days of the assault. He saw the bruises, the *harm*, and it pisses him off that the charges have been reduced. Sexual assault within a spousal relationship can be difficult to prove, so it's not surprising that it was stayed. The same might go for unlawful confinement. But what about the weapons charge? According to the police report, Nolin had an unregistered handgun and threatened to use it on Marina and on them. With the evidence of the gun itself, how could that charge have been reduced?

It does a probation officer no good to puzzle too long over the actions of lawyers and judges. Sometimes the outcome of the legal negotiations or a trial can make the PO's efforts seem like a waste of time, but the same might be said in other jobs. A degree of detachment is helpful, perhaps essential, for sanity's sake.

Detachment and sanity, right. Of course, he can't stop thinking about Marina. The presence of her lovely face, deep eyes, olive skin, athletic body, and little webbed toes have taken his imagination hostage. He's doing everything else with about half his mind, the part still rooted in reality. But as he shuffles the paper on his desk and collects his thoughts to begin the report, having this chapter of Marina's life documented in a cardboard file seems surreal. Nothing is impossible; Fate proves that over and over. And so the significance of his own name can conceivably shift from a supposedly detached official to what police call a "person of interest" in these very running record notes, on this lined legal paper, when someone else will handle the file in future. That scenario makes Peter more than a little nervous.

He phones the prosecutor's office to speak with the senior secretary, a font of information. "Lynn, what's with the Nolin case? Five major charges reduced to two and even those have been amended?"

"Well, Sydney Schaeffer's his lawyer, for one thing. Something tells me Daddy's picking up the tab on this one, because apparently Todd Nolin's blown everything he made playing hockey." Lynn leans into the phone. Peter hears the rustle of her collar against the receiver as she continues, now whispering. "So Schaeffer flies into town a week ago, and he's in our office within two hours with Nolin. He's a great big fat guy, you know, and likes to throw it around. Basically, he says his client will plead to lesser charges right then and there if they can agree on a recommendation for sentence and all that. But if they leave the office without a deal, then his client will plead not guilty across the board, with expert witnesses brought in, plus a couple of local boys who have some interesting testimony about Ms. Faro."

"What?" Peter almost shouts. "What kind of tactic is that?"

"That's big league, Peter, and the Crown on this one, Alan McKay, he knows Schaeffer has an all-star batting average. Schaeffer hates to lose. He rarely pleads a client out, except when the deal amounts to winning, and he's paid enough. That's what I've heard."

"But expert witnesses? For what?"

"The crime-of-passion angle, some psychologist, I guess. You've read Faro's statement? Nolin was out drinking with his buddies, found out his girlfriend engaged in a little ménage à trois while he was out of town, and flipped his lid. Not surprising, if you think about it. Schaeffer might have even got an acquittal, but he's a big-city guy and probably didn't really want to spend the time here required for a trial."

"Sometimes I think I'm in the wrong business, Lynn."

"Well, don't forget it is *business* in many cases."

"Thanks for the insight."

"You're welcome. I know you mean well, Peter, but just write the report and let it go. You've got a has-been hockey player, along with a tramp, by the sound of it. Sprinkle a little cocaine around, what do you expect?"

"Thanks again," he says.

So Peter can never say he wasn't warned.

On Wednesday mornings the office closes at ten for half an hour, and most of the staff members go out for coffee together to a little restaurant three blocks away. Often Peter opts out, preferring time on his own in the empty office to the coffee klatch, with all the doughnuts, town gossip, and opinions. They have a culture he hasn't quite fitted into yet, and since Karen left, Peter has felt even more solitary. But he doesn't want to alienate himself, either, and the cinnamon buns are pretty good fresh out of the oven.

So he follows them one Wednesday, trailing the pack as they walk along on a bright blue morning, past a few houses that are among the oldest in town, with big trees in the yards, leafy willow branches arching over the sidewalk. He notes the garden tools, wheel barrows, and little back sheds.

Woodgate is near the front of the group, his tall frame lumbering along and his grey crewcut a head above the rest. Tammy and Jean, the admin team, flank the manager, and the three are laughing about something. Greg Milchem is beside Jasmin Jassal, aka "J.J.," playing up their professional intensity. She's the latest criminology grad to join their ranks, and just so happens to be a knockout, which is a torturous combination for Milchem. In his own mind he has so much street-smart wisdom to offer her, and no doubt a foot massage if she'll let him. When Peter's in good humour, Milchem's babble can really amuse him, but at other times it can be an annoyance.

By contrast, Don Robinson is the consummate PO, both for his systems expertise and in his manner, be it with co-workers or clients. He's extra well dressed this morning in an olive-green blazer and probably has a court appearance sometime today. Barry Martens is an ex–jail guard who transferred to Community Corrections more than ten years ago and secured a PO job prior to the current criteria for education. He fancies himself something of a cowboy, red sideburns, boots, and all, and his bulk and mentality serve him well when it comes to steer wrestling or facing hostile clients who, in his words, "need a tuning." He's tight with Woodgate, and like the boss, eyes Peter and his less-than-macho ways with suspicion.

Altogether it's a fairly honest, average bunch of people walking ahead of him with whom Peter shares little but the commitment to the job, which does mean something. For quite various reasons they all believe in what they're doing.

"Hey, you decided to join the gang today?" a voice from just behind surprises him as Laine catches up and matches Peter's pace. She's the exception to the conservative rules of the others as she lights a second cigarette off the butt of her last. "Wanna smoke?"

"Ah, sure, thanks," he replies, conceding to the craving. He generally keeps his own cigarettes in his vehicle.

They halt their steps while she produces a lighter, and he leans in to the flame she holds. Laine must have a closet full of black clothes, because she rarely wears anything else. Her garb, smokes, and gruff manner belie a sensitive nature, and she's the only one of the crew Peter has ever had any personal rapport with, although not recently. Maybe it's simpler because she's gay and their connection has been free of sexual tension. Peter finds wry irony in the fact that he's often been on good terms with lesbians, up to and including the one he married which, of course, was unknown at the time.

"You've done a good job avoiding me, Peter, but I have ways of making you talk," she says in a bad German accent.

He grins a bit sheepishly, and she frowns back so fiercely while blowing smoke out her nose that he laughs outright for the first time in a long while. Then he sighs. "I know. It just seemed easier, but I hope you didn't take it wrong. Though I admit I was a bit pissed off at your whole alternative gender there for a while. Do you think if I'd offered to have a sex change Karen might have stayed?"

"Ah, nope. Besides, that's messy and complicated. You don't need it, pal."

"Well, what if I'm really a lesbian in a man's body?"

Laine snorts. "Well, that's a different twist, and in your case maybe not entirely out of the question."

They stop again outside the restaurant to finish their smokes. Elaine Perault did her degree in social work and worked with what used to be called delinquent kids, then moved to Adult Corrections. She, too, had once been married, in the early nineties, lived in Vancouver for several years, obtained a job with probation in the city, and met a woman and a community that altered her path in life. When she applied for her current job, Woodgate was unable to conceal his discomfort, his neck and ears colouring in any conversation that strayed from the straight and narrow. But he had to abide by union rules, and she was by far the best-qualified candidate. He quickly found her to be a great asset to the team, a crackerjack report writer, and a reliable PO. So the small-town office adjusted, and Peter admires Laine for her courage.

"Feels like it's too early in the morning to get into the subject, Peter, but let's make a deal," Laine says in her leather jacket, hanging one boot over the curb.

"Maybe. What's that?"

"Sometime soon, whenever you're ready, let's go out and have a few beers and shoot some pool. Then you can ask all the crazy questions you want, and I can pretend that I know what the hell I'm talking about when it comes to relationships. Okay?" She butts out in the concrete bird bath full of sand that stands beside the door.

"Okay," he says, and follows suit.

Karen put a high value on health, and their life together included whole grains, tofu, and a regimen of exercise, biking, and hiking. She took this consciousness with her to California, and Peter has fallen into one bad habit after another with sullen defiance. He drinks too much coffee, often instant in the mornings, has taken up smoking, and buys frozen pizzas, canned chili, and alcohol.

The house is neglected and shows it, but damned if he can rouse himself to tidy things up. Somehow it's the contrary zone he's in, reacting to the clean ways of their life before as a defence against missing it to the point of angry despair. The kitchen radio plays the local country station, which Karen abhorred, but Peter can sing along to the heartbreak tunes at the top of his lungs if he wants to now. Garth Brooks has got nothing on him. Peter can stack the Budweiser cans right on the counter and not worry about anyone coming to visit. One more evening finds him sitting on the back deck in a weathered chair facing west, puffing on the last of a cigarette, a vodka tonic in the other hand, irritated by his own base pleasures.

Shouts cross the yard from the neighbour kids playing ball hockey in their driveway. He recalls that the spring season always coincides with the NHL playoffs, now in progress. The sound of scraping sticks propels a distant memory forward. He was never very good at hockey, but of course he played it. And that was as close as he ever came to taking part in any team sport, those faraway spring evenings, because he never belonged to a school team or any other. The idolization of athletes and their astronomical salaries has always struck Peter as bizarre, say, in contrast to the starvation of children and the persecution of freedoms around the world. He can't guess which teams will vie for the Stanley Cup, or which one will win, and he doesn't care.

Nope, Peter has never been very competitive himself, never a sports star, nor a capitalist. Yet neither has he escaped or been thrown out of the game to date. But as Dwight Yoakam sings, *Baby, things change.* He holds a university degree, but has an insecure and paltry-paying job. But now that job's at risk because he's gotten himself involved with a woman by way of business. His intended life partner, better half, ski bum pal, ex-wife, and soulmate is now long gone. He's losing his house, this house …

Peter gets up, walks out onto the concrete parking pad in his bare feet, and lights another cigarette. He feels a bit like a little plastic figure in a game of Monopoly or Life, falling behind, waylaid in common pitfalls, with no dignified way to simply quit. He paces in a slow circle while the sun lingers low in the June sky, then plucks a few dandelion heads between his bare toes.

Next door the boys are right in the thick of the hockey game, their voices and sticks in pursuit of the orange street hockey ball flying back and forth. Even in slow adult motion, Peter sweats in the evening air. Knowing how easy it is to screw up, how suddenly one can fall, trip, and go down, knowing how hard it is not to lose control of the ball.

chapter fifteen

The pre-sentence report interview with Todd Nolin is set for three-thirty on Friday afternoon, so as to least disrupt the man's work schedule at the store. After the preceding hours spent dealing with court process paperwork, cranky clerks, and challenging offenders, Peter is a bit weary. He's staring out the window when the phone rings and Tammy informs him that Nolin has arrived.

Peter gathers the loose pages lying on his desk into a legal manila file, picks up a notepad and a pen, and walks out front. After greeting Nolin rather coolly, he leads him to one of the barren interview offices, the one adjacent to Woodgate's.

"Have a seat. I realize this is time away from your workplace, and I won't take any more of it than necessary. Maybe an hour."

"I already spent an hour filling in this form," he complains, putting down the standard questionnaire given to clients to complete prior to a PSR interview.

"Okay, so that's two hours of your attention to the matter. It's rather important."

He smirks. "Maybe to you."

"Mr. Nolin, the purpose of a pre-sentence report is to give the judge some idea of your background and the circumstances that might have led to the offence. In fact, you've pleaded guilty to two criminal offences on the good advice of your lawyer. These will be convictions on your record. Most people don't take this as a laughing matter."

"Are you saying I do?" Nolin thrusts his torso over the table. "Am I laughing?"

"No, you're not," Peter replies as calmly as he can, hairs rising on his neck. Inwardly, he groans at the ordeal ahead of him, listening to this gorilla for an hour without resorting to violence of his own. He recalls Marina talking about Todd and rules, how they only provoke him. It's a simple enough observation, which Peter has made himself of other clients many times before, but it fits Nolin especially well. "Would you care for a glass of water?"

"No! I'd care to get on with it and be finished with this bullshit."

"Okay." Peter opens the file in front of him, pulls a notepad close to hand, and picks up his pen. "I hear you're quite a hockey player. Weren't you drafted by the NHL a few years ago?"

Peter tries every strategy in the book to put Nolin at ease. Motivational interviewing, it's called. He puts extra effort into it, anything to compensate for the fact that his own contact with Ms. Faro puts him, Peter *Halfwit* Ellis, way the hell out of bounds and in a serious conflict of interest with the subject of this PSR. But there's no way to get out of doing the report now, not without provoking Woodgate or raising suspicion. So by way of careful questioning, he gets Nolin to tell his story.

Todd Nolin is the youngest of four children from the marriage of Sandra and Gary Nolin. He has three older sisters, the youngest being nine years Todd's senior. The subject speaks well of his childhood, with obvious pride that his father has been financially successful. As the youngest and the only son, Mrs. Nolin suggests that "Todd has always been the apple of his father's eye."

Gary Nolin has worked over thirty years in the automotive business, and since 1998 has owned a share of Big Country Nissan, a local auto dealership. Sandra Nolin played a large hand in rearing their children. She has worked in real estate, but chose to stay home during Todd's preschool years. Mrs. Nolin was a willing contributor to this report out of evident concern for her son. Mr. Nolin declined to be interviewed.

Todd Nolin had academic difficulties in school and was suspended several times for problematic behaviour. However, by the sixth grade his athletic abilities were noticed by a sports-minded principal, and by the eighth grade he gained some notoriety. A newspaper article of the time described him as follows: "The premier Junior A player in the north half of the province with potential to go all the way." During Todd's eleventh year at school, he transferred midway through the year to Medicine Hat so that he could join and bolster their promising Junior A team. Within three years Todd was drafted into the NHL by the Buffalo Sabres, which remains a defining moment in his life to date.

During the off-season, he returned to live with his parents in his hometown. By this time, Gary Nolin had become co-owner of the Nissan dealership. The Nolin family held considerable status locally. When Todd returned home, at least during the period he held an NHL contract, according to collateral sources, he was viewed as a hometown hero. After the expiry of his contract and the end of his brief professional hockey career, he no longer held this status.

When Nolin finishes with the details of his life, Peter says, shaking his head with just enough admiration to maybe put the guy off guard, "Well, that's something. Not many guys can say they played in the big league. You were what, twenty years old, bought your own house here over in Westridge, right? Say, do you still own that home?"

"Are we getting down to the *really* stupid questions now or what?" Nolin swivels sideways to look out the window, as if maybe he's finished talking altogether. "Why would I be living in a condo if I still owned the house, huh? There's a question for you."

"I thought you might have rented the house, with your mother as agent perhaps. She mentioned she sells real estate. As for the apartment at Arbour Villa, I wasn't sure how —"

"I sold the house because I couldn't make the payments. Is that what you're after? Yeah, I made some money, I spent some money, big deal. I own a share of the store. I'm not fucking bankrupt. What's your point?"

"Well, not to belabour it, but you did have a sizable income for the duration of your contract. And you say you 'spent some money,' so can you tell me what you spent it on?"

Todd Nolin began drinking alcohol in his mid-teens and experimented somewhat with drugs. The subject views his own experience with alcohol and drugs to have been quite ordinary among his peer group. By the age of seventeen, he was entrenched in a pattern of binge drinking on a weekly basis. This ceased, at least for a time, with the advances of his hockey career and the demands of professional athletic training. However, his sizable salary also gave him newfound access to a wider choice of substances.

The subject was guarded throughout the PSR interview, but especially in discussion of this topic. He did disclose his use of cocaine, which began approximately four years ago. He admitted to using cocaine on the night of the offence, which brings him before the court, and on several occasions since. Again he apparently saw nothing unusual in this behaviour and questioned the connection to this report.

Collateral sources have informed the writer that Mr. Nolin has been a frequent user of cocaine and various amphetamines in recent years and has often had substantial amounts of the narcotics stored at his residence. Mr. Nolin vehemently denied this.

The subject disclosed habitual use of alcohol and the fact that he is often intoxicated twice a week.

Their discussion of alcohol use does cause Peter some guilt, seeing as he's now commonly intoxicated himself most evenings. He's taken up cigarettes with a vengeance and has even been smoking some crusty yellow marijuana he discovered in the course of packing boxes to ship off to Karen. So really he's in no position to judge Nolin's addictions.

"Can you give me some background on your relationship with Ms. Faro?" he asks.

"Background?"

"Well, how about whatever you think is most important?"

"You want to know how we got together and all that?"

"Not necessarily."

"Well, I didn't marry her for her cooking, if that's what you mean. Whatever else she is, Marina's pretty hot for a small-town girl. Even in Buffalo, for that matter. Or maybe you've noticed?" Nolin seems amused with himself.

Peter has his head down, ostensibly scribbling notes, and ignores the inflection of the last question. In such moments he's not averse to exercising his authority. Instead he takes a breath and asks, "And you lived together over the past two years until recently?"

Nolin smirks again. "Until you guys got involved, yeah."

He must mean the justice system in general. There's almost no way on earth he could know anything about Peter's contact with Marina — other than the fact of her beauty and body, the male instinct that many other males will want her. Still, Peter has a flash of worry. Nolin's insolent gaze sends up a red flag, a silent inner alert.

Todd Nolin and Marina Faro entered into a relationship approximately three years ago. In contrast to Ms. Faro's account, covered elsewhere in this report, Mr. Nolin denied that his behaviour had become increasingly abusive during the previous year. He said that Ms. Faro's unhappiness in the relationship was due to her "personal baggage," a term he repeated but wouldn't specify. He also repeatedly questioned why she had stayed with him if she was so unhappy. When the writer suggested she might have feared for her safety, the subject openly scoffed.

At no point during the PSR interview did Mr. Nolin volunteer any remorse for his offences or empathy for the victim.

When asked, he went to some length to rationalize his actions, and at several points returned to Ms. Faro's infidelity as though it provided his justification.

"So what would you do?" Nolin asks. "You're out at a bar and you overhear this guy talking about some fox at some party. The guy says she went with him and a friend into the laundry room and fucked them both. Her name's Minnie, or Marnie, no, Marina, that's it. She's living with some guy. And guess what — you're the guy! How would you like hearing that?"

This statement interrupts Peter's focus on the interview. For a moment his imagination is diverted, with Marina in the laundry room, her beautiful face flushed with booze and coke, her body contorting as required.

"Makes you think, huh?"

"I'm sure it was troubling news."

"Fucking troubling news. Yeah, you could say that. Your girlfriend turns into a slut. No normal guy's going to take that!"

"She didn't 'turn into' anything, whether or not the incident took place, or whatever happened. Has there been any infidelity on your part?"

"What do you mean?"

"During the past three years, while you were living in Buffalo maybe, have you had intimate encounters with other women?"

Nolin tilts his jaw to one side and sneers. "Intimate? You don't have any idea, man. I'm sure you'd be interested to write it all down, but forget it."

"So you did have encounters?"

Although Mr. Nolin minimized the importance of the loss of his NHL contract and denied that his own reckless actions on the ice had anything to do with it, collateral sources suggest this had a marked impact upon his life. In the course of a few months, he lost both status and salary, and this transition might have affected him more than he realizes or will acknowledge. It marked an increase in his substance abuse, and during the past year, there have been numerous episodes of erratic and violent behaviour. This included increasingly abusive treatment toward Ms. Faro. She has stated that in the months prior to the offence she feared for her life. Considering Mr. Nolin's explicit threats on several occasions, and his considerable size and strength, her fears appear well founded to the writer.

The subject has no previous criminal record, however he was known to the police from a previous investigation. This information is included herein because the incident was of a serious nature, similar to the present one, and the writer believes it was a precedent for the current offences. The assault of Ms. Faro was not an isolated incident, but a peak in a pattern of abusive behaviour that had been escalating for some time.

Lack of victim empathy such as Mr. Nolin has exhibited isn't uncommon in cases of spousal assault, however the degree of his defensiveness and his repeated attempts to justify his actions are unusual. Also unusual is the fact that he expressed amusement or scorn at several points during the PSR interview. For these reasons it is recommended that, if Mr. Nolin's sentence includes a term of community supervision, the order include a condition to attend, participate, and complete a forensic psychiatric assessment at the direction of a probation officer.

The door of the interview room is half-open. Peter glimpses Tammy and others packing up for the day, Woodgate strolling out the door, and figures that's good reason to end the interview. He's heard enough for one sitting. Nolin exits with no pleasantries.

Peter walks back to his desk with the report file in hand and tucks it into the cabinet, along with a couple of others lying on his desk from earlier in the day. He leans over the keyboard to sign out on the computer, drops his pen in its holder, and turns to leave. The phone rings, but he walks away, eight steps, ten, until the voice mail activates. Then curiosity reels him backward to check the message.

"Oh, hi, this is Marina Faro calling back. I got your message about the interview for the report. I've told you most of it, I think. But I'd like to talk, so maybe we can tomorrow? Thanks."

The computer clock reads 4:55. Peter cranes his neck around, then takes a few steps down the aisle and back just to be sure he's alone. Finally, he returns to stand and stare down at the phone.

chapter sixteen

After five on Friday afternoon, Peter paces around the empty office twice like a bear in a cage, returns to his desk, and stares at the phone once more. He picks up the grey receiver and punches out the number he knows by heart already, but which is forbidden to him after hours. He hangs up immediately after the first ring.

Five minutes later he's driving across town, slowed by more traffic than usual because it's the first weekend in July, the start of the Stampede rodeo. Ball tournaments, concerts, beer gardens, and general exuberance are in command of the town. After sitting in the sun all day, the Bronco's cab is an oven, and he's got both windows wide open to the scents of sage and diesel and the rising din from the streets. The rusty old beast coughs in second gear, and Peter mutters with impatience.

What is the power of attraction? None of the biological factors really matter anymore, do they? Is our culture peaking with confusion, or just as primitive as ever? Who am I? These are thoughts that cross his mind in random sequence.

Peter doesn't view himself as handsome or ugly, but something in between. He's content to fall within the bell curve, among the great masses of the lopsided. But for Marina, her athletic, feminine body and a face that lets others, mainly men, see whatever they desire must be a burden on her at times, Peter surmises. And for him, what, a quest? He's seen her driving around town in the agency Camry, literally turning heads. His connection to her is suspect in every way, his motive, his ethics, or glaring lack thereof, and it will probably cost him his job.

Driving under the speed limit, he's free to take any turn and head home, away from her. On the job he shies away from much counselling with probationers, but it always seems safe to remind them of this point: Everybody has the power of choice. You can choose to go this way or that one and live with the consequences. Yet right now he's ignoring that choice, or for the moment he feels he has no choice, and so what safety lies in the truism?

What he does is select the alley closest to her apartment, easing down it until there's a spot to park, to keep his Bronco out of sight. He locks up the vehicle and then takes a short path through the weeds to the back of the Arbour Villa parking lot. His stomach is knotted as he scans the lot and yard, slows his pace, takes a few deep breaths. And makes it to unit 5 unseen, as far as he can tell.

Marina answers the door, holding what he takes to be a chocolate bar at first glance. She finishes chewing, compressing her lips, then says, "Oh, hi." Marina seems surprised, which makes him fear it's all in his head.

I'm going crazy, he thinks. *Take a breath, ten, nine, eight, seven.*

"Working overtime?" she asks him.

"I got your message at the end of the day. Thought I'd just stop by and make sure everything's okay."

"What do you mean?"

Peter sees from the bar's wrapper that it's one of those ultra-energy snacks. Marina's Adidas and little white socks are on the doorstep. Her face is still for the moment, and he has no idea what she thinks of him standing there. She might tell him to get lost and stop harassing her, that she's phoning his boss. Instead she smiles, backs into her kitchen, and says, "Come in."

She's wearing running gear — a loose muscle shirt over a sports bra, dark ocean-blue shorts, bare feet. Those curious toes look perfect. He's reminded, from previous visits, that the rooms visible to him tell little about her. The furnishings are quite new; everything is tidy and clean. She asks about his day, and he mentions the interview with Nolin. "It made me understand what you talked about a bit better at least."

"Try living with him for two and a half years," she says, taking a last bite of the bar, then opening the cupboard under the sink to discard the wrapper. He stands empty-handed in the entrance. She walks past him toward the living room and throws herself onto the blue leather couch. And he makes another choice, to follow her, and slips out of his shoes. "I *can't* understand him, believe me, the fact that he likes threatening my life, as you know."

Just for a moment Peter wonders: is this overtime? Then he reminds himself that he's here after hours for no justifiable reason in his socks of his own would-be free will. And his mouth all at once goes dry, his jaw and throat somewhat numb, as if an invisible dentist has just stuck a needle under his tongue. Marina is talking.

"Todd isn't stupid, but he doesn't think like most people. I mean, he just doesn't understand the limits. As far as he's concerned, it's all about him, and no joke. You think he's sorry about what happened a month ago? He's not. As far as he's concerned, I deserved it. And so why won't he let me go? Relationships go wrong, people split up, it's not even unusual. A close friend of mine broke up with her boyfriend a while ago, and he was hurt, sure, very hurt, I guess, but he had some basic decency. He didn't beat her up."

Peter nods for lack of a better response, works his cotton mouth, then finally says, "There's a question we're not supposed to ask, probation officers, I mean, but it's crossed my mind in your case. What you describe more or less answers it."

"What? How we got involved in the first place, or why I stayed with him?" She arches her brows as though in challenge. "From what you said before it doesn't sound like your marriage was made in heaven, so I take it you're not judging me."

Peter shakes his head, sitting now in the blue leather chair opposite her. "Not at all. You see, that's why the question's taboo. One simple reason — life gets crazy sometimes for anyone." He hears himself sigh, then half laugh at himself.

She turns to face him, places one bare foot on the carpet, the other on the coffee table. "But just so you know, the first year or so was pretty good. For one thing we didn't see that much of each other when he was away playing hockey, and when we did, sometimes it was Toronto or Buffalo or Vancouver. It was a bit unreal. He only moved back here because his contract wasn't renewed after he was sent down to the minors. He was stressed out about that, but he was partying like he was already a millionaire. I participated in that, yes. He said I 'looked the part.' That's what he said, and it wasn't my first clue of chaos coming by a long shot. Then he had to sell the house in Westridge, unload it, really, because he couldn't make the payments." Marina stands and walks into the kitchen, picks up the cat's empty water dish, and fills it at the sink. Then she paces back and forth between the rooms, raises her arms, swings them wildly, hair lashing the air. "Of course, I should have walked away a long time ago!"

"Listen," he says, "I'm not here for any explanation …"

"No, I don't blame you for asking."

"But I didn't ask."

"After his contract was done, he wasn't a Buffalo Sabre anymore. He wasn't going to be an enforcer. That's what he talked about, raved about, when he got loaded. At first I tried to support him. And after a while I thought maybe I was only part of the problem. So I tried talking about that, very carefully, mind you. And when he figured out that I was suggesting we might separate, he flipped, of course. It was the first time he threatened me, I guess. He was drunk, but he said he'd take me to a taxidermist and have me stuffed so I could stand naked in the corner of the bedroom like a good girl before he'd let me move out! Then he laughed and wanted sex. After that I was just plain fucking scared of him. He's built like a gorilla. Look at me! I said look at me!"

Peter did and opened his hands, a weak gesture of understanding.

"I weigh one hundred and eighteen pounds," she says, moving her hands like a figure skater in the finale. "So for the past year or so I've lived with that ape, God forgive me. And it's screwed me up. I've lost touch with my family, my mother.

I can't even talk to her yet. I had to sleep in the same bed. I had to sleep with him …"

Her voice falters, and Peter tries to think of something to say. He feels a deep stab of guilt, listening to her, because his interest is well beyond professional courtesy. This history she's telling reveals more of her identity, which he readily accepts, drawing closer to her.

Marina slumps back onto the couch and covers her face for a moment. "Since I've been alone, even after six weeks I can see how screwed up I was living with him. That's why it took something bizarre to break free. Do you see? It had to be something he couldn't live with. I don't know if you believe that, but that's how it was for me. I'm not making excuses for what I did."

She brings her knees together and lays her hands flat. "It became too frightening to be with him. I couldn't really sleep, not knowing what he might do snapped up on cocaine. Eventually, though, he'd pass out. Then I'd have a few hours of peace." She sighs. "And do you want to know the worst thing?"

"Only if it's something you need to say."

She pauses, nods, then whispers, "The worst thing is I actually thought of killing him. Can you believe that?"

"Yes," he says slowly, "I'm sure that thought isn't uncommon in such a situation. In fact, some women carry through with it."

Marina stands abruptly, braces one arm straight against the wall, puts one bare leg out in a runner's stretch, then the other. As if she has to move in some way to distance herself from what she's told him. She ducks her chin, and her glossy brown hair parts over the nape of her neck. "Sorry, all of a sudden I got a cramp."

"You were out for a run?"

"Just a short one, right after work. It helps clear my head. Do you run?"

"Not for some time. Maybe I should take it up again." He smiles, thinking, yeah, in between cigarettes. He feels unhealthy and decrepit next to her, simply because her body has the harmony and perfection of a deer or a porpoise.

"I have to meet a couple of girls downtown in a while."

"Oh, I'll get out of here then." He stands and turns toward the kitchen.

"There's no panic. It's not until later on. I didn't mean to unload on you like that. And I'm not chasing you out."

"I just wanted to be sure all was well here with you," he says, his jaw going numb again, fiddling with his shoes, backing up to the door, his hand on the knob. "I have to, ah, go buy some chicken or something. Find some dinner. Maybe chow mein. Chicken chow mein."

"Chicken chow mein?"

"Yeah, do you like it? I do with a bit of sambal olek. You know, the hot sauce?"

Marina smiles, then starts laughing outright at him. "Yes, I like chow mein. And I guess I'm okay. I'm doing better than I was, anyway. Getting there, you know. But I'm glad you came by, Peter."

"Okay, take care." He's turning the doorknob now. She's still smiling, with a twist, and it's a good way to exit.

"Hey, before you go, there's something maybe you can help me with. This way." With that abrupt suggestion and a beckoning finger, she heads back through the living room.

Peter can't stop his own feet, forgets he doesn't have his shoes. Perhaps she needs help with a light bulb or a dripping tap. He follows her ocean-blue shorts up the carpeted stairwell.

Halfway up, her fingers take the hem of her T-shirt and peel it over her head, the sports bra with it, and she turns, facing him from two steps above. Her hands land on his shoulders, and they kiss. Marina's skin is warm to the touch. His mouth travels down her neck, over her shoulders, her breasts and belly. Her fingers are in his hair, unfastening his shirt, belt, and jeans. He touches her shoulders, her arms, and her body's voltage runs through his own arms and chest, making him gasp. His fingers splay over her back, trace the indent of her spine to her hips, the elastic hem of her shorts, which slip away.

Marina is balanced on the stair above, her thighs lifted, cradled now in his hands. He brushes the smooth muscle of each thigh with his fingers and tastes the light spice of sweat left from her run. Her breathy voice urges him, and his mouth moves upward, over the rich dark hair and warm skin of her pubes. She throws her head back, and he feels the sounds rising from within just before he hears her throat vocalize, a sweet laughter of surprise and thrilling sexual joy.

Peter's next clear thought is about an hour later. Lying in bed with Marina, he watches her sleep, her deep, even breaths swelling the sheets like the gentlest surf. He runs his hand over his face a few times, pushes fingers back through his reddish mop, and wishes he had a stiff drink. *Really,* he thinks, *let's face it, friend. This situation is out of hand. The proverbial frying pan into the fire, all systems alert.*

A cooling breeze passes into the room, bringing the scents of summer grass and distant sage, and he feels strangely calm. Every muscle from his scalp to his toes is relaxed and warm. She rouses slowly, stretching, though her eyes remain closed as he studies her face. Karen has a beauty that still makes Peter's heart clench when he recalls the character of her face, the allure not everyone saw. But Marina's beauty is bold, even reckless, in the curve of her full lips and cheekbones, her dark brows, and her eyes. She's so vulnerable to the world's gaze. And for the second time in a minute his chest constricts, this time for a new woman in his life. Her presence takes hold of his heart like a sail catching a breeze.

"Hmm." She sighs and turns her face to him with a sleepy grin. "Are you still thinking about chicken chow mein with hot sauce? You seemed a bit obsessed."

He laughs softly at himself and all else. "I'll take what you offer anytime and gladly starve to death."

"Oh, what time is it?" she whispers.

"Seven-thirty something," he says quietly, touching her shoulder, combing back her beautiful chestnut hair with his fingers.

"Oh, then I'm running behind." She smiles, raising herself, accepting his kiss. Then she places her head on his chest. "I wish we could stay like this, or better yet, wake up in another room far, far away, with nothing else to think or worry about. I am sorry. It's my friend's birthday party at this restaurant, and I helped organize it, so I better show up."

"Of course, don't be sorry about that." He kisses her again, his heart doing a sudden plunge. "Maybe I'm the one to apologize. I mean, what am I doing here crashing into your life like this? I shouldn't have come."

"Which time would that be?" She chuckles, slapping his belly as she sits up and swings her feet to the floor.

Peter rolls out of the bed, too, and gathers his clothes. She stands naked, stretches her limbs, and heads for the shower. He catches her hand. She turns into him as his fingertips softly rain down her back, circle the dolphin tattoo on her hip, and settle on the curve of her ass. "Are you still okay?" he whispers.

"Yes, I am, more than okay." She kisses him with gusto, her dark eyes trying to read his face. "Are you?"

"Yeah," he lies.

chapter seventeen

The light has softened only slightly when he leaves her door. The world looks slightly different than it did three hours earlier, but he knows the change is in himself, that danger still lurks in the bushes. He scans the yard of the complex and strides along the walkway. Just before he gets around the corner of the building, he hears a door open behind him. Thinking it could be Marina, he glances back, but it's old Mrs. Kubova in unit 6 getting a good look at his guilty face.

He makes it to the Bronco and nearly floods it in haste. The engine groans but doesn't fire, the starter whining. He jams his foot to the floor until the poor thing bursts into life, farting black smoke. "Come on, baby, don't you dare."

Peter's pulse races, and though he's perfectly sober, he doesn't feel it's safe for him to drive. Suddenly, he's hungry, too. Not for the first time today he's afraid he's having a breakdown, as if a great hand is shaking the puzzle box of his brain. So he begins to look for a place to park and decides on a spot in front of a dental clinic. The Bronco sticks out like a sore thumb scabbed with rust on the empty side street. It's Friday just before eight o'clock. Peter rubs his face vigorously and climbs out for air.

A warm breeze carries the effluvia of the dry evergreen hills, the lake and creek fringed by reeds, wild grasses and sage and weeds, all this mixed with urban smells, mainly exhaust from all the traffic in town this holiday weekend. He takes it all in with deep breaths, leaning against the Ford until his heart settles down a bit. Up the greener end of the street toward the cemetery a tumbleweed skitters across the pavement.

He's forgotten the appetite sex can bring on. Notwithstanding the fact that this entanglement with Marina is so far out of bounds it makes his head spin, he's now hungry like a bear following his nose. The handiest establishment is the café in the Trailhead Hotel, serving Chinese and Western cuisine. He hasn't been there for a long time but recalls the sweet and sour soup as pretty good. So he starts with that and a beer. About half the booths in the place are occupied, mostly by Tsilhqot'in and Secwepemc folk. A large table at the back is crowded with the owner's extended family, the food and discussion passing back and forth in Cantonese.

Peter lifts his hand to signal the youngster serving him. "I'd like combo three with the chicken chow mein and prawns, please. Oh, and a bit of hot sauce on the side."

"Another Molson?"

He nods. "Sure, thanks."

After the meal, he has a double cheap Scotch for dessert. The fortune cookie reads: "A sunny disposition will reap its own rewards."

Peter finds the café a good place to sit and reflect, sipping his drink. People are enjoying life all around him, disadvantaged or marginalized as they might be. It doesn't seem to matter much to them at the moment. The summer light gradually lessens outside in the dusty street. Karen is maybe attending some string quartet mime performance on the beach scene in California. Marina is out with her local friends, and he desperately hopes not to encounter her tonight in town. That's all too possible now that he's half-drunk and won't be making that twenty-minute drive home. So he has no place to sleep, but that seems the least of his worries.

The little round cup of green tea begins quivering on the tabletop, alerting him to deep thumping elsewhere in the hotel, from the Corral bar where the band has started playing. He pays cash with a five-dollar tip, and the youngster smiles goodbye. Then he exits the café into the inner hallway of the old building, which boasts antique felt burgundy wallpaper in a floral pattern suggestive of an old-fashioned whorehouse, and truth be known, it's not only decor they have in common. This hallway leads via a few turns into another, a rougher, sloping rubber walkway that empties into the bar.

Peter immediately finds comfort in the place on this loud Friday night that kicks off the Stampede weekend. Almost two years have passed since he was last here, but it smells the same. It's known as the "Indian bar" but is also popular with all races of bikers and loggers, wayward cowboys and assorted women, and drug dealers. It's only a matter of time, about half a minute, before Peter recognizes a probation client who might be breaching conditions just by breathing the smoky air. *But to hell with that,* he says to himself. *I'm here and I'm going to have a drink or two and an evening truce with the criminals.*

The bar is a bulwark of dark wood, a worn counter lined with jars of pickled eggs and sausages, a hot dog machine, and the three industrial chrome spigots that spew out the draft beer. Men are queued up reaching into their pockets and over the bar, and Peter takes his place in line. The guy beside him shows the bartender two fingers and receives two glasses of draft in return. Peter glances over the noisy bar and sees that no one has a mug in front of them, but pairs of singles, and recalls that they buy it this way because for the same price they figure you get an extra two ounces of beer. This not only suits his purpose at the moment, but when in Rome … He raises two fingers and shells out his money. No tables are empty, but traffic along the bar is fluid enough that gradually he works his way along to the shadowy end where he can lean against the wall and order more draft.

Every song the band plays sounds a little like ZZ Top, whether it's one of the longbeards' own or Randy Travis's. And that's okay. It gets people dancing. In the shadows with his back to the wall Peter isn't in a position to judge, not a figure of authority, but a man messed up in a questionable relationship, drinking. Shifting his gaze around the room, he recognizes several more persons known to him from work, clients of the justice system, their pairs of empties in front of them. He recalls why he liked this joint in the past because, apart from the general exuberance of character, it's a place that asks no questions, though he's getting curious looks from a few of those clients. He has no answers and feels in no way above them, but more than a bit conspicuous.

After almost two hours and half a dozen glasses, he feels plain drunk and more vulnerable to the crowd. A fight breaks out at the edge of the dance floor, and the bouncers roughly dispatch both parties through the double front doors to the curb outside. The commotion stirs Peter from his seat, and he angles for the back door he came in. Violence unnerves him even when sober, so right now he must escape the scene. The rubber walkway seems a steep climb toward fresh air, and as he reaches the outside, he hears someone behind him. Peter walks away, his balance slack, and finds himself in a maze of motorcycles, Harleys, where there's the hazard of tipping one or two over and then being chained and dragged screaming down the street by outraged bikers. He sidesteps out of this booby trap and leans for moment of relief against the faded blue wall of the old hotel.

"Have you been drinkin'?" someone asks, whoever followed him out, standing half-hidden in shadow. The voice is familiar, the context blurred. Then the tall figure reveals himself — Levi Charlie with grinning eyes.

"Oh, Mr. Charlie, you caught me." Peter grins sheepishly, runs a hand through his hair, and tells himself he's not really drunk, but he is. He braces himself against the wall. "The salmon … have you been fishing?"

"I don't fish much, I told you. Not every Indian's fishin' all the time."

"Of course not. I didn't mean it that way," Peter says, then laughs at himself. "Levi, I'm afraid you've got me in a compromised situation here. I came for some chow mein, one thing led to another, and now I need air. I think it's the MSG they put in the food."

The old guy chuckles. "Yeah, sweet and sour pork, bad habit."

A bit stooped, slim as a Jack pine, Levi wears his usual purple bandana, yoke shirt, faded Wranglers, and boots worn down at the heel. Tipped back on his dark scalp is a black Coors ball cap. Levi threads his way out of the gravel lot, maybe drunk, but steadier in step than Peter at the moment. He stops and turns, and with a mere glance backward, invites the younger man.

So Peter follows, catches up, and matches pace, passing along a quiet street in the older quarter of town. After a bit, he wonders where they're going. Levi clearly has a direction in mind, which is more than he could muster right now. Still and all, this guy has a long-standing criminal record and is currently under supervision on bail for a charge of assault. Levi's stride isn't hurried, but steady enough that Peter has to work at keeping up. Breathing deeply, he hopes to settle his stomach and clear his head.

At the end of the street Levi keeps walking into untended ground, knee-high grass and sage, and finds the outline of a winding trail under a summer moon.

"Where are you headed, Levi? I could buy us a cup of coffee over at Denny's, but that's in the other direction."

"Maybe later. First I'll show you somethin'."

"That's what got me into this fix, a suggestion like that," he mutters to his drunken self beyond the old guy's hearing.

As they angle down a steep slope and Peter braces his arms against the bank to avoid injury, he realizes they're nearing the rodeo and fairgrounds. He's just sober enough to marvel at Levi's balance. They approach from the back, which takes them by a series of fenced paddocks and a row house of box stalls, with the horses turning watchful eyes on them. Eventually, they come to the corrals holding the rodeo circuit stock, calves, steers, and broncs milling together in the largest grass area, and farther on, the sand and sawdust plot holding fifteen or more bulls, Brahmas, Longhorns, and Angus, behind a higher reinforced fence. Levi rests his forearms against the fence rail and surveys the animals.

"That one," he speaks quietly, pointing a leathery hand at one of the humpbacked, long-eared Brahmas. "He reminds me of Double V, the last bull I rode. Same crazy look in his eye."

"Yeah, I see what you mean," Peter says, gazing at the muscle-laden frame, weighing maybe two thousand pounds, flared nostrils, its head crowned by thick, curved black horns. Levi used to climb on top of such creatures, holding on to nothing more than a rope in one hand and his faith, and spur the massive shoulders. Peter tries to imagine twisting through the air aboard the fuming giant. "Those are good memories, Levi?"

The old man nods. "Good memories." He stares at the bulls in silence.

Peter is familiar with this silence, with Levi, and others of his people in interviews, which are sparsely worded. Sometimes, as with Levi, it's as if they communicate telepathically, if one listens. And Peter has tried to listen.

"Oh, Levi, I'm in a mess," Peter confesses, leaning against the fence and bowing his head against the cool top rail. He tries to focus on the ground.

"You're drinkin'."

"Yes, that's a fact, but the whole thing's a bit more complicated."

"Always is."

"This involves a woman."

"Always does."

Peter tilts his head to look at the old duffer, his sombre, dignified face, and Levi cuts his eyes sideways just long enough to reveal the hint of a smile. And more silence.

"Wasn't *complicated* ridin' bulls," he says, "but the same fear, yes or no. You always have a choice, that's probation, don't you always say?"

"Yes, that is, in fact, what we say."

The old guy turns his head away as a striped white car swiftly rolls toward them along the gravel lane beside the barns. A patrol car, Constable Bergstrom and his partner on night shift, with a spotlight freezing them. "Good evening, gentleman. These grounds are closed to the public. Mind telling me what you're doing and how you got in here?"

"Hello, Officer," Peter pipes up. "Say, ah, I didn't realize that. We came in from Birch Street, and we didn't cross a fence or anything."

"Other than jumping down the bank, you mean?" Bergstrom asks, swivelling the spotlight. "Say, where do I know you from?"

"Hard to say," Peter says, then sees his folly. "I mean, probably the probation office. Yeah, I work over there. The thing is, I'm acquainted with Mr. Charlie. Through the office."

Bergstrom studies him, unrelenting, unconvinced. "Yes, in fact, you're trespassing in his company. He's well-known for this sort of thing. And I have to ask if you've been drinking alcohol tonight."

"Some, yes." Peter nods, takes a breath, and braces his hand on his knee, peering into the car. "The thing is, it's after hours certainly, and these are questionable circumstances. But we met in a restaurant, by coincidence, and we've been discussing a bit of a situation. We were just walking, and I had no idea this was off limits. It isn't normally, is it?"

"Well, *the thing is*," says the smart-ass officer, mimicking Peter's slurred excuses, "it's after midnight. And it's closed to anyone without a rodeo permit to be camping down here."

"Is it?" Peter says. "Well, there, you see, I had no idea. Though we were just heading over to Denny's for a coffee."

"You're going to climb that hill out of here?"

"Right away, oh, yeah," Peter says, rubbing his hand over his face. "Right away."

"No, I'm afraid not," Bergstrom says sternly, glancing across at his partner and shaking his head. "You understand the concept of public safety, I take it? And I'm thinking the safest place for you two tonight is a jail cell. You can be released on bail tomorrow for trespassing by night and report to your own office on Monday morning, but on the other side of the counter. How do you like them apples?" The officer pulls on his black gloves, which adds some effect.

This scenario sobers Peter considerably, a heartbroken outlaw out of luck in the hands of a righteous posse. *See, Karen*, his soul cries out. *See what I've come to!*

"Forget it! Fuck, man, you're loaded." Bergstrom laughs and shakes his head at the other officer. "Climb in. We'll run you over to the restaurant."

Peter turns, his relief like a charge of adrenaline. He gives Levi a hidden thumbs-up over his buckle and opens the rear door of the cruiser. "Mr. Charlie, our taxi's here."

From the back of the police car, Peter stares out as they roll through the Stampede grounds, pull onto the highway, and accelerate up the hill into town. Moonlight and neon dapple the sagebrush slopes and the slough at the outflow of the lake, while light pools farther out on the black water. Old Levi keeps one hand braced against the handleless door as if he's used to this procedure.

Peter awakens to the clip-clop-clip-clop of horses' hooves on asphalt and finds himself lying on the back seat of his Bronco, boots on, legs bent, with no feeling in his left foot and a searing backache. The windows are open a few inches for air, with sunlight and sounds of the day coming in. He raises himself on one elbow with a groan to look out, then ducks his tousled head right away in case he might be seen.

A trio of riders — three girls on gleaming quarter horses, a bay, a buckskin, and a sorrel — pass by in full rodeo regalia. Their boots shine, their tight jeans press to the saddle leather, and they wear matching turquoise blouses embroidered with feathers and red thread, their hair flowering in curls from beneath white straw Stetsons. Each girl carries a flagstaff with the banner furled for now, the butt of the pole fitted into a leather cup attached to her stirrup, her polished boots heels down, and the horses' strong, dark legs marking rhythm.

The parade assembles in the side streets where most shops aren't open yet or are closed for the day, such as the dental clinic by which Peter chose to park last night. He lies low in the back seat while various other segments of the parade make their way toward city hall: beribboned floats pulled by polished antique trucks, others set up on lowbeds behind Kenworths and Western Stars, big diesels rumbling, more horses, draft teams, a school band all dressed in green and white, the bicycle club, the gymnastics club, show dogs and llamas, and this year's special guest from Saskatchewan, Ringo the trained Longhorn. All these and more, plus loose bands of giddy children, and families, many adults holding fast to their morning coffee.

Coffee, he thinks, *can't think very well without it at the best of times.* And water, he could really use some water. Acetaminophen, too, might help. He leans into the front of the cab and rummages through the glovebox, finds a plastic bottle that rattles with three pills, and swallows them dry. Then he pops some chewing gum and settles back onto the rear seat to let a wave of dizziness pass.

Lying very still, a bit fearful, he tries to retrace the sequence of events from the night before. *A sunny disposition will reap its own rewards.* Sweet and sour soup, the Corral. Did he tip over a Harley? No, that's where Levi found him. It's all a bit fuzzy, but he remembers Bergstrom's white face and red moustache well enough. He might have ended up in jail, and the way it is, even a rumour of what happened could cost him his job. And then he slept here in the Bronco. It was a better choice than driving, but with the keys sitting there in the ashtray, he could still have been arrested for being under care or control of a vehicle while intoxicated. In the business of probation, or from most perspectives, these are called bad choices.

Marina … She's got that blue dolphin tattooed on her hip, the left, no, right. The creature is about the length of his own fingers caressing it. He knows full well he's under a spell and can't cast it off. He's forgotten that it can happen like that — headlong into the loop of intimacy. No choice, though. Her sea-lime scent still lingers on his skin.

chapter eighteen

Friday evening they parted too hurriedly without much discussion, and Peter is left to endure a long weekend with no means to be in touch with Marina. He can't call, with the police tracking her phone contact, and going by there again is out of the question. The worst thought is that she'll regret their intimacy and take that out on herself. She's vulnerable, and he hasn't considered any consequences, walked right into this dream world, one encased in hostile territory called reality. He feels a nausea that won't go away. There's no one else to talk to about this. He does think of Laine, but no way. That would put her, too, in a bad spot.

On Tuesday morning he answers his desk phone. "Peter Ellis."

"Hi, Peter Ellis," she says. He rolls his chair back to check the corridor, to note the nearest desks are empty for the moment. Then he turns toward the window and leans into the receiver, as nervous as a schoolboy, in a quandary of hope, guilt, and expectation of disappointment.

"Are you there?" she asks a bit louder, and laughs, her voice sounding personal.

"Yes, how are you doing?"

"Better than I have been for a while, but I missed you this weekend."

He sighs. "Yeah, I've missed you, too."

"I'd like to see you. What can we do? Have you thought of a plan?"

"A plan?" He can't help but laugh at that. "Can't say as I have, no."

"Do you know Mary's Diner, that truck stop about half an hour south on the highway?"

They meet there at seven that evening, and he leaves his Bronco parked at the back of the lot. She's borrowed a friend's car, and she drives another few minutes down the highway before turning onto a country road that leads to a single picnic site beside a cattail pond. Peter feels a bit like a rooster in good hands, sitting in that Honda, fixated on Marina's beauty, pleasantly amazed by her resourcefulness.

She turns off the ignition, twists toward him in one motion, and they embrace. Soon the car is too cramped, and they end up utilizing the picnic table, with a beach towel laid out to protect her back. Her body's rhythm puts him into a long trance, surrounded by whispering aspens and lush green growth along the shore. Afterward they sit on top of the table on the red terry towel, gazing out at the still black water glowing in the sun. Marina may be vulnerable, but she's assertive and full of life, seemingly at peace with him. Sitting there in silence for a while, they can smell the teeming life of the pond.

"Good plan you came up with," he says softly, pulling her into him.

"Yeah, well, it's your turn next time." She laughs and pushes him down on the table.

He follows her back to town, watching her closely at the wheel of the car ahead of him, and she waves in her rearview mirror as they part company in town. On Thursday evening she takes a cab to a service station where they meet and drive north this time. The best he can do is a highway motel. Their bodies are new to each other and hungry, demanding.

"It feels like I've known you before, though," she says softly, "like I'm remembering this from another lifetime?"

"Hmm, which century?"

"Oh, I think you were a pirate." She laughs, and her voice gently ties him to her.

Another night in another motel she imagines a castle, mirrors, candles, and a canopied bed.

"What's that word for those fancy frames on pictures and mirrors?"

"The frames?" He chuckles, watching her eyes, her imagination in gentle flight. "Ornate?"

"The gold ones?"

"Oh, gilded."

"Yeah, like that, ornate gilded mirrors," she whispers.

In this economy room, beige walls, synthetic blankets. Another woman and man following chance. His age and sadness threaten until she begins to move her fingers over his skin.

Peter can't claim a long list of past sexual adventures. He had a few girlfriends in his twenties, one at a time for the most part, and too often he fell too fast in love. Too sappy, a buddy once suggested. It interferes. The relationship with Karen came to mean everything to him. He was faithful to her, and they kept up the passion. Yet a part of him wasn't surprised by her eventual change of heart and preference. At one time or another they talked through every subject under the western sun, and for some time he knew she had a growing interest in women. So Peter has been in and out of love, but not for quite sometime. He's fascinated by a woman's effortless power to captivate him, maybe too romantic, too trusting. Each time it's like walking a wire from risk toward trust, in his gut a compelling hunger that makes him take one step, then another.

Being with Marina, though, is like jumping from a plane into a twenty-foot surf, one of those hybrid extreme sports, like nothing he's experienced before. She's ten years younger but knows her body and what pleases her, and lets him know, sometimes in an eager whisper that blinds him to anything but her want. Falling in love with her is absurd, but almost a fait accompli, and a complicated fate. The taste of her skin fills his mouth. She's in his dreams, follows him from night to dawn, and is there in his mind when he wakes every morning.

They haven't talked in depth about where it's going, because there's no place for it to go, no route open. Both can see that. Defying all sense and his own will, Peter's imagination has created scenarios, including a different town, a different job, as his hold on this one is precarious, anyway. Try a different century and a covered wagon, or a different planet where they live happily ever after as sea creatures underwater. The desire between them is as tangible as fruit, like a table laden with pineapples, bananas, and mangoes. But one drawn by Salvador Dali, with the table set in the middle of an airport runway or an open-pit mine.

On a Sunday afternoon they manage to get out of town once more, drive west and south, and hike for a couple of hours in a desert canyon. Peter has packed a lunch of cheese and grapes, along with a little green bottle of wine. It's a beautiful sunny day, fragrant with sage. They follow switchbacks of the trail up a steep slope, and he watches Marina climbing gamely ahead of him, nimble and without hesitation. This is the first time they've done anything like this together, and it doesn't feel forbidden for a while, but like something amazingly simple. They pause now and then to catch their breath, and she calls him over at one point to look at a small flat cactus in bloom with tiny yellow flowers.

The other side of the ridge is crested with golden dunes. They find a sheltered hollow among them, throw the blanket onto the warm sand, and make love at first in frenzy, and then slowly forgetting time for a while.

Later they sit out on the dune under the sun, eating Swiss cheese peeled out of foil and sipping the wine from plastic cups. At first they talk more freely than before, about this and that, ordinary things without consequences attached. It pleases him to make her laugh and to see her lovely smile. Across the steep valley are sandstone hoodoos and high banks swooping down to the green river below. Peter imagines traversing such a face, how one slip would send him into a plunge, and sitting beside Marina, his heart feels a similar sense of vertigo. The landscape is stunning, and they grow quiet taking it in. After a few minutes, though, the nature of the silence changes. They become lost in separate thoughts, each self-conscious of the other sharing the view and the blanket. Too much of a picnic all of sudden, a bit happy-go-lucky, all things considered.

"I've been thinking of moving away for a while," Marina says finally.

Peter nods. It only makes sense. "For how long?"

"Oh, I mean, it's been on my mind for months, or years, leaving town, moving somewhere else. And the other day I just realized that nothing's stopping me now."

"No," Peter says quietly without meeting her eyes. "It only makes sense. Do you know where you might go?"

"Probably Toronto. Last year I began studying for my level-one licence, and the company sent me out there for a week of training. Then things got crazy with Todd, or crazier, I should say, and I haven't completed the exams yet. But I've stayed in touch with one of the women from my class, and she keeps asking when I'm coming back. She got her level one, and she says there's lots of opportunity. I doubt I can transfer, but I can get a good reference and maybe find an office with connections to the same company."

"Yeah, that makes a lot of sense," Peter says, summoning enthusiasm for her, repeating himself for lack of other words, shutting up the fool inside him that can make her no better offer. "I'm sure you'd do very well."

She smiles. "If I put my mind to it, I will. And it's time to get a grip on my own mind. Besides, it doesn't look like Todd's going to jail, does it? I can't remember the last time I didn't wake up at night terrified just knowing he's out there, doing what he wants. So the farther away for me the better."

Peter gazes across the dunes, the wide, rugged canyon, and big green river, a very long way from Toronto, knowing there's no going back for himself.

chapter nineteen

It's mid-July and the Stampede is two weeks past, but the dust has yet to settle. On the hills the sage soaks in the sun with dry joy, with the odd errant plant selected by nature to break free and roll along the highway. And where the highway turns into main street the tourist caravans follow the tumbleweed through the junction intersection, along the upper rim of the bowl where the rodeo grounds lie, where Levi Charlie and his friends, with hat brims shielding the light, discuss the Western body politic in their own language and pidgin English, CN trains rumble north south with lost boxcars from Wisconsin tagging along, the Russian olive trees flourish just as the city's landscape consultant said they would, where bumper stickers declare this town's allegiance to beef and trees for slaughter, where not counting the franchise strip, welcome visitors have a choice of seventeen restaurants, six of them specializing in Chinese and Western cuisine, twenty some churches, including the House of Hallelujah and a Sikh temple, the goodwill of India, a town where the Angels deliver drugs and visit now and then, where one will find brochures with paragraphs in German and Japanese, but customer service costs extra, the kids dress like rappers like anywhere else, where almost everything is imported, much of it not long ago, the vote remains conservative, Hollywood comes knocking, and the mayor's wife drives a silver Hummer.

"Peter?"

He swivels around from the window to find Don Robinson standing beside his desk. "Hey, Don."

"I don't know if you've heard, but I got the job in the East Vancouver office."

"The pilot drug project? No, I didn't know. Hey, congratulations!"

"Thanks, yeah, I'm looking forward to it." Robinson wears a white shirt and wrinkle-free blue slacks, every inch the professional. "You've been keeping to yourself lately. I know it must have been a bit rough. I mean, since Karen left, but you're doing okay?"

"Oh, yeah." Peter is actually touched by the question, but laughs it off. "Away to the city. Good for you."

"Yeah, this is my last day, in fact. I booked holidays for the next two weeks, but now that I'm moving, Woodgate gave me the go-ahead. With me gone you'll have a better shot at a permanent position, if you still want that."

"Permanent, what a word," Peter says, standing and extending his hand to Don. "All the best."

"To you, too, Peter."

Don brims with goodwill and justice as he steps up the ladder. He's tailor-made for the bureaucracy, not a bad guy considering that, but he's always made Peter feel like an imposter in the job. And never more than at the moment.

A haircut for Peter is in order, or was about six weeks ago. Running late this morning again, he brought his razor to work, then left it in the Bronco, he realizes now as he scratches his jaw. He drank too much last night again, the vodka bringing on a slow narcosis. But it was either that or seek out Marina. He hasn't seen her for three nights now. All along he's told himself: *You're out of bounds, boy. This is nuts*. And on Sunday, with the news of her plans for Toronto, they seemed to be on the same last page of their story, which in long hours since has brought him untold heartache. *Let her go. Take the high road*. The fact that he can't call her at home, with the police trace on her line, has meant no long, drawn-out conversations.

The desk phone rings, and it's Tammy. "Mr. Bail Supervisor, you've got two clients out here at the counter. I rang the bell myself twice, like five minutes ago. Naptime's over."

Thursday when he arrives back from lunch break the office is buzzing. Milchem, Martens, and Woodgate are talking over one another in the office common, with Jas Jassal listening.

"Like lemmings," Milchem says. "Same sort of thing."

"Come on, it's a stupid place for a road!"

"Lemmings?"

"They should block it off or fence the edge or something, for God's sake."

"It's public land. So any steps they take, even to prevent people going over, would make the district liable if it ever happened again."

Martens grins at J.J. "Them little gophers that live in the Arctic."

"Classic, cover the collective ass by doing nothing. Leaving the public at risk."

"Yup."

"Anyway, what I can't figure is who gets drunk and says, 'Hey, let's see how close we can drive to the cliff edge'?"

"These kids! It happens about every five years, doesn't it, George?"

"Indeed."

"The guy wasn't a kid. He was twenty something."

"Who?" Peter asks, trying to cut through the cluster of conversation.

"The poor bastard who drove his truck into The Ashtray last night," Martens says. "Tammy heard it from the cops. News was just released."

"Anyone we know?" Peter asks.

"Client?" Milchem says. "Nope. Apparently, it was a brand-new truck. He must have been working. Sounds like he was well-known, a popular kid."

"Suicide maybe?" Peter suggests.

"Police aren't saying much," Woodgate says. "Probably can't tell at this point. Sounds like it took them all morning to get the truck hauled out of that gorge. They'll be down there with the coroner and the accident team."

Peter shakes his head, then heads back to his desk where numerous files needing work await him. Approximately one hundred at present, but at any given time there are a dozen new ones requiring the step-by-step procedure, many long-term, low-maintenance files, and then those in crisis, causing calls to and from social workers, addiction counsellors, police.

Todd Nolin is due in court next Wednesday for sentencing. Peter is counting the days, wanting the matter over and done with. He questions the report he wrote, or the point of the exercise. Sometimes the PSR has some effect, often not. As Marina fears, it's quite possible Nolin won't get jail time but a community order, thanks to his high-priced lawyer, and if so, Peter is bound to see him in the office on a regular basis. And he doesn't relish that prospect.

Peter feels each hour passing since he last kissed Marina. Over and over he tells himself: *This is the way it is, full stop. Don't fool yourself.* It reminds him of adolescence, the hours of mooning over teenage romance, the doubt and private midnight declarations. Trying to contact her through imagination alone, willing his thoughts to reach just that far. Picturing her in bed. There were moments with Marina that he'll never forget, that he might recall every night for the rest of his life. Her face above him, her breasts touching his face, her body in his mouth. Peter would like to think, but can't believe that Marina feels anything like he does for her. But the most important thing now, right now, for both of them, is that no one ever knows. *I know, she knows.* It was all wrong, from any angle. Even so, he's heartbroken and shaky for the second time in less than a year. Life is just too much goddamn fun.

And death is a reminder. He thinks of the young man found this morning in the gorge, The Ashtray, in the crumpled wreck of a shiny new pickup. He recalls Marina describing the night many years ago when her first boyfriend stepped over that same precipice. Extended his arm, to catch himself, and was gone without a sound.

The phone rings. "Peter Ellis speaking."

"Hello, I'm calling about Steve McCauley. I'm his wife."

"Yes, Ms. McCauley, how can I help you?"

"It's missus, I just told you. And we need him home. This is his place, and there's about forty jobs need doing."

Meanwhile Peter draws the file from a drawer, checks the bail conditions, the record, a couple of impaired driving charges, one previous spousal assault that was dropped. "I see. You have a copy of the bail order? Okay. No, well, no, I don't have any experience raising cattle. But I understand it involves a lot of work. No, yes, you're right. If you want to change the conditions of the order, you need to contact Crown Counsel, and they'll consider an application to vary. Yes, I have the number."

Peter summarizes all this in the file's running record and slips it back in its place in the drawer. Then he opens the top drawer of his desk and finds a stick of gum. Three minutes later the phone rings again. "Peter Ellis speaking."

"Hello, Janice here," the police court liaison says. "Just to let you know, Yvonne Lemaire is in custody."

"Oh, yeah, what's the latest?"

"Last night she was chasing somebody around the Goldpan with a pool cue. Charged with breach of bail, assault causing harm, and resisting arrest. She's going to be held, looks like, over the weekend and appear before a judge on Monday."

"Okay," he says, drawing another file from the drawer. "Sounds like that's in the public interest, generally. Thanks for letting me know."

"One less on your mind for now."

This is the way he charts the chaos, the lives he makes note of, and Peter doubts whether he can make any difference. Be decent and respectful, or try, even when the other party is lying, or minimizing his sex offence, or outright telling him to go to hell.

Shortly thereafter the phone rings again. It's now twenty after four, and he's going to let this call go to voice mail, which is reasonable. He'll deal with it tomorrow. But just as the third ring subsides, something occurs to him, and he picks up the receiver.

"Yes?" he asks as if he were sitting at home, half surprised by the call. He never answers at work in this manner.

"It's me, Marina."

"Yes …" His heart swells upward.

"Did you hear about Rick?"

"Rick?" he asks, now hearing her panic.

"A friend just called to tell me. Rick Cusson, they found his truck in The Ashtray. He …" She begins to cry.

"Marina …" A finger of frost climbs his spine. Her voice and breathing is frantic. "Where are you?"

"At work," she says, "for another twenty minutes. Then what? I'm not going home."

"And Rick Cusson?"

"He was one of the guys at that party," she says, anger rising, knowing he knows. "And Laurie, my friend, told me she saw him with Todd last night. They were drinking like nothing ever happened, she said."

"Okay, Marina, the police will look —"

"They'll look into it tomorrow or next Monday, you mean! He killed him! I know it. He told me he would, and he did. He killed Rick!"

For a moment it seems far-fetched until he recalls where she's coming from, how Marina's first boyfriend died. Nolin knows Marina's terror of the cliff site. He *knows* what this would do to her, and the brutal logic is chilling.

"I'm leaving now," he says. "I'll pick you up. I'll be there in five. Marina?"

"Okay."

Peter heads for the rear door of the office. "Tammy, I forgot I've got a dentist appointment in two minutes. Gotta run."

"Hey, wait, who's closing up?" she calls after him, but he's already long gone.

chapter twenty

The halting afternoon traffic delays him. Six minutes, seven, eight. The sun beats down, glaring off window glass, reverberating off the asphalt in waves. To save going around the block, he makes an illegal turn onto Third Avenue. The light is yellow at the next intersection, red as he passes through.

Marina is standing outside in front of the agency, and when she sees him coming, she steps off the curb in her sundress. He brakes, and she climbs into the Bronco. They have never met like this, in public daylight, in the middle of town. Instinctively, he scans the sidewalks for anyone who might recognize, take note.

She's wearing the same green dress she wore the first day he met her, the one she changed into the colour of ferns, the hem at mid-thigh as she fastens her seat belt. Her face is drawn, her eyes red as they briefly meet his own full of concern. A horn honks behind him, and he lurches the Bronco forward. She crosses her arms, tucks her chin against her neck, breathes deeply. "I think I'm going crazy. I do. I'm going crazy. And that's what he wants. I know it."

"Marina, what happened to your friend, we don't know yet that it wasn't an accident. That's what it looks like, according to the police —"

"What do they know? I'm fed up with the police, and the lawyers, and the judge that lets Todd be out there doing whatever he pleases. He beat me, he threatened me, Peter, and if you had seen him that night, you'd know that he meant it!" Her voice is raw with both anger and fear. "And Rick wasn't my friend. God, I barely knew him. He was a hockey buddy of Todd's. How could they be out drinking last night like old times? Todd swore he was going to kill him, and I'm sure he did somehow."

"You told the police that, too? I don't recall the threats against Rick from your statement. And there was another guy involved?"

"They interviewed me three or four times! I told them. I told the prosecutor. The other guy at the party was from out of town. I can't even remember his name."

"Then the police will look into that. I'll call them as soon as we find somewhere safe for you." Peter reaches over and places his hand on the edge of her seat, not touching her but offering, as he stares through the windshield, working his jaw.

After a moment, she takes his hand. "Thank you for doing this. After what we agreed, you know."

"I know, but you know something else? I'm glad to be with you. I mean, Marina, these circumstances aside. Listen, why don't you come out to my place just for tonight until we've talked to the cops and we know where Todd is? I'll sleep on the couch, promise, cross my heart."

She ducks her head and shakes it at the same time, her beautiful hair curling in a wave over her bare shoulders. But there's at least the trace of a smile on her face, which streaks through his chest like a jolt from one of those coronary recharge pads. Peter realizes this situation is off the map, yet he feels he's where he should be.

"I need to get a few things from my place, at least a change of clothes," she says.

"Yeah." He wheels the Bronco into a turning lane, heading toward Arbour Villa.

Inside her apartment he stands in the kitchen while she slips off her shoes and trots upstairs. She's eager to get out of there. He doesn't blame her for being upset, though the Nolin killer theory still seems a bit far-fetched. They know nothing for certain.

Peter walks around her kitchen. On the counter beside the stove he notices a small ceramic dish holding half a bulb of garlic, and other little jars of dried oregano, and so on. Peter hasn't pictured her here with a wooden spoon in hand, and smiles at the thought. He paces once around the island, then moves into the living area. On his earlier visits the decor wasn't foremost in mind, but with a few minutes on his own he studies each object for whatever it might tell him about Marina. Above the gas fireplace there's a mantel shelf bearing an empty glass vase and a few framed photos. One shows her as a girl with a dark-eyed woman, clearly her mother, on the deck of a ship or ferry with their hair windblown. Another is of an elderly couple standing in the midst of a knee-high vegetable garden. The other photos are more recent, but in none of them does he find a man likely to be her father. He recalls each and every time they've talked, but there's still so much he doesn't know. Lying in the motel room dark after making love, she's been sometimes guarded, other times childlike, always returning simply to the woman in his arms. And then gone.

He moves to the window and checks the street. It's only been a few minutes, but he's growing impatient. Taking her out to his place is crazy, out of the question, so why did he suggest it? Change of plan: she can go to the women's shelter at least for the night. The closer she gets the more it's going to hurt him again. *Okay, so that's settled.*

Above there's a thump on the floor and a bang. He whirls away from the window and is up the stairwell in about six driving strides, checking room to room. "Marina?"

"What?" Her voice echoes his alarm as he reaches the bedroom door.

"Oh, Christ, I heard something ..."

"Just that stupid suitcase. It fell when I pulled it off the closet shelf." She gestures at it behind her on the floor. Various clothes are laid out on the bedspread. Quickly, she transfers these to the open case, in no pattern, then grabs an armful of little socks and stockings from the open dresser drawer and throws them on top. She's changed into blue jeans, but no top yet, still in her white lace bra. She's either too distracted or familiar enough with him as a lover not to care that he's watching her. Her haste, her hair tossing, and the angry set of her mouth pierce his chest.

"I'm sorry."

"For what?" she snaps, bending to close the overfull case, fighting with the zipper.

"For barging in on you. Here, let me do that."

He steps forward, leans over, presses the case flat with one hand, and zips it shut. Marina sits back on the bed, drops her hands to her thighs, and begins to cry. Peter kneels in front of her, and after a moment, she wraps her arms around his neck. For a while. He's afraid to move, his hands resting on the swell of her waist, the scent of her skin and hair making him a little dizzy, her elixir.

He feels her lips move against his ear, and the desire he's fought for weeks runs through his arms like heroin, like fire through his fingers curling against the waist of her jeans. And she whispers, "Maybe just for tonight?"

Peter exhales a slow breath, laughs softly, finds her lips wet with tears. "We can go to my place. We should."

Then his mouth is roaming over her neck, her shoulders, her chest. With a simple movement she unfastens her bra, sitting upright, and his eyes caress her breasts for a half a moment before he moves in hungrily on her swelling nipples. Marina sighs, her voice shifting from anger and sorrow to desire within these past few moments, drawing him as close as he can be, will ever be, to her heart. Her heart beating there beneath his open mouth.

She lies back on the bed, and her fingers, with the clear polished nails, unfasten the brass button of her jeans. He leans over her and presses his mouth to the bared lower muscle of her belly. Slips his fingers into her back pockets and tugs downward.

Her belly is as pure as a fresh clay vase. Her body has perfect symmetry and tone, a muscular vibrancy. Peter feels like a shipwrecked sailor, isolated, ragged, but by blessed chance sitting down to eat fruit with the natives, and then offered an island princess, or offered to her. She takes command, seizes his arms and back in her hands. The actual nondescript room, the circumstances, and time itself are gone. She wants him inside her. She's talking to him, asking, laughing. She grabs his hair roughly in hand, and leaning down, swears into his mouth. Peter laughs softly and does as he's told. He kisses the blue dolphin tattoo on her hip in passing. Instinctively, he knows that this woman has changed his life, for better or worse, and this aching knowledge drives him into her.

At some point they drift near sleep, wrapped together. Then she gently rouses him, and after a short while, he moves over her, listening again. Their differences, their stories, their names fade out of the room. Peter has never truly believed in time, the conventional version, that is, partly because sex takes him so far beyond it. Good music does something similar, transforms minutes and hours, but not quite like this. Skin to skin, breath for breath.

Peter feels Marina's hand on his shoulder, and for a moment before opening his eyes he lifts his own hand to find hers. But her touch has changed, now urgent in a different way. She's sitting up, one foot on the rug, then both, reaching for her jeans. "I heard something, like someone at the door."

Still lying back against the pillows, Peter inclines his ear. "Your neighbour's TV. I can hear that. That old guy needs a set of earphones."

"No, something else."

This something is icily clear in her tone, and Peter rolls out of bed an instant later, pulling on his khakis, tipping into the wall. Marina grabs a top at random from the scattered pile.

Downstairs there's a crash, a chair hitting metal, denting the fridge or stove, a slurred voice cursing. Down on one knee pulling his pants on, Peter gets a glimpse of himself across the bed — wild hair and hands, scrambling in the dresser mirror.

"Oh, *Jesus Christ*, it's him!"

"Marina?"

"Peter," she whispers, leaning toward him, "stay here."

Before he fully realizes what she's said, what she's doing, she walks out the bedroom door. In a hoarse whisper he cries, *"Marina!"*

She's gone down the stairwell. She's greeting the bastard that just broke into her house, the son of a bitch who's threatened to kill her. "Hello, Todd. You know you're not supposed to be here."

"Hey, nice to see you, too, Marina. Very, very nice." Nolin sounds drunk or high, maybe both.

She stands at the foot of the stairwell, looking at Nolin across the room. Peter pauses at the top, and she doesn't shift her eyes, but raises her hand from the railing. A signal to him, concealed from Nolin. She has some strategy in mind already and moves forward into the room out of Peter's sight. "What's the gun for, Todd?"

"Nice, huh? They call it a 'bear buster.' It holds seven twelve-gauge shells and fits on your backpack." He laughs. "I found it stashed in the office closet at the store. Good old Dave."

"But you don't need that. It's not too late to put it down and leave. I mean, take the gun away. I won't say a word. You're going to court next week, and we can put this behind us."

"Well, fuck me, aren't you little Miss Common Sense all of a sudden."

"Everything can be settled, Todd. It doesn't have to get worse."

Peter has inched his way down to the second-from-bottom step, his back pressed to the wall. His body has gone from slumber near sleep to all systems alert in the past half-minute. His forehead and neck are beaded with sweat; his heart is pounding in his chest and ears.

"Did you hear about Rick?" Nolin asks Marina. "Poor guy. Anyhow, that's settled, I guess. Yeah, and now this, baby. This will settle everything else." He jerks the slide back and forth on the shotgun and points the muzzle at her. "That fucking PO. He drives a piece-of-shit rusty Ford. And now it's, let's see, 6:40 p.m., and that Bronco's parked out in the lot plain as day. So where is he?"

"Todd …"

"Where is he?"

Her scream begins, and a saving instinct makes Peter turn a split second before the bear shot bursts through the plaster three steps above, and another load nearer. The blasts propel him face first against the wall at the foot of the stairs. Plaster dust, debris, and gun smoke cloud the room.

Peter rolls out of his fall, pushes his bare feet off from the wall, and launches himself across eight feet at Nolin's staggering bulk. "Marina, get out!"

Nolin swings the black barrel like a hockey stick and splits Peter's right ear before they crash backward into the cosmetic mantel and gas fireplace, glass doors shattering. A third blast goes upward through the ceiling. At the end of their fall, for just a moment, Peter has the advantage, but his punch is slow, easily deflected by Nolin. They roll in the glass on the carpet. He catches a last sight of Marina, hesitating in the open doorway. Nolin swings the shotgun. Peter twists and lands a kick against the knee holding his weight. Nolin screams and brings the weapon down against Peter's face.

chapter twenty-one

Consciousness brings pain at the best of times. But never before has Peter experienced the excruciating red-capped waves that now sweep over him one after another, breaking through his skull like a windblown tide crashing into a cliff. He feels as if he's drowning, has fluid in his throat, and it's his coughing that brings full awareness. His nose is swollen shut, his throat disgorging blood and phlegm over his chin. He tries to lean forward, then to lift a hand to clear his mouth, but multiple bands of clear packing tape bind his entire torso so that he can't move.

Light strobes steadily through the room, red and blue, and his hearing returns with a whoop, different frequencies, emergency vehicles circling the site. Fluorescent life. *Thanks, God. I owe you. I'm alive. My, oh, my Jesus fucking Christ, this pain.* Blood drips off his chin. Sweat frosts his forehead, runs between his eyes.

A scraping noise causes him to turn his head toward the kitchen. Nolin has hauled the kitchen stove over against the door. Lying flat on the floor, he kicks it into position with his right foot. No mean feat, juggling words and meaning, Peter's brain venting, clutching at any diversion from the present. Amazingly amused, he snorts like a stuck pig, more blood. At the sound Nolin flips over on the floor and reaches for the shotgun, their eyes meeting over the line of the barrel. It's black, blunt, the muzzle wavers. But not enough to matter. From ten feet the discharge could take his throbbing head right off. For an instant of perverse hope the thought offers relief.

"So you're not dead yet." Nolin grins. "That's okay. I started thinking you might come in handy."

Peter considers and decides against silence. Nodding toward the kitchen entrance and white stove jammed against the door, he slurs through swollen lips, "Expectin' company?"

"Sooner or later, yeah. But that's where you come in." Nolin's grin softens. "It was hard not killing you. Blasting you like a fuckin' gopher. But I think you might just get us both out of here, alive, I mean. What do you say?"

Any reply is a strain for Peter, but his shattered face does its best to look optimistic. "Right. I can … can do that."

Nolin crawls diagonally across the living room, favouring his left leg, the shotgun in his right hand. His dark hair is close-cut. He wears black athletic pants of synthetic material, a grey knit T-shirt, the latest silver Nikes, and he looks quite natural crawling like a lizard with enamel eyes. He gets to the foot of the stairwell and the narrow vertical window, where he slowly lifts his head to look outside.

"I count three cop cars, an ambulance, a black Tahoe covered with aerials. Must be more fucking cops. And what have we here? Looks like a TV van! Shit, I'm famous again.

They'll have other cars out back." Nolin turns with his back to the wall below the windowsill, an overeager player assessing the opponents. "We're definitely the underdogs."

Peter snorts at the understatement, growing nauseous with pain along with his mental forecasts of various scenarios. A dozen wraps of plastic packing tape prevent his body slumping with his goddamn spirit, remind him that he's essentially at the mercy of this two-hundred-and-fifty-pound homicidal cuckold, who just a short time before discovered Peter half-dressed with Marina in her bare webbed feet.

"So?" Peter ventures, this smallest word painful from his damaged lips.

"Hah!" Nolin rolls over and over across the floor to halt in front of the big chair Peter's tied into. His pupils are fully dilated, glossy black. He chops the barrel of the shotgun across Peter's bare feet. "So we've gotta focus on our strengths, what we got that can stop their offence."

Oh, Jesus. Peter winces, tries to think of what to say. He imagines the building ringed by high-powered rifles, and here he sits in a potential crossfire while this chemically fired ape lives out his Rambo fantasies, rather wisely staying close to the floor.

"That's you, dude, the hostage." Nolin laughs vigorously, and Peter thinks maybe from coke, maybe some new millennium pro-athlete speed, along with whatever booze he's consumed. Also maybe from the unavoidable fact that his life is ruined now and he's running the last available bluff. *That's me.*

His captor crawls to the next window, back into the kitchen, to the rear window over the sink. From a crouch he grabs the microwave from its inset counter and props it on its side on the windowsill, apparently as a fireguard. He checks the fridge, slams it shut. Then, from an upper corner cupboard, Nolin extracts a brown bottle of rye, and after placing the shotgun on the counter, unscrews the cap and takes a lengthy drink, "Ah! There we go. She never liked the hard stuff, eh? As far as I know. Maybe you know different, Mr. Bail Supervisor. Have her tastes changed lately?"

Nolin has the shotgun in his right hand, the liquor in his left, and somehow coordinates his crawl across the floor toward Peter, dragging his left leg, the muzzle of the weapon lifting nearer and nearer. The black hole of the shotgun rising, closing in, then jutting in at the base of Peter's breastbone, the steel barrel breaking skin and maybe the windpipe. Peter coughs blood and twists his head in panic, feels the chair slide slightly with his shifted weight.

"What do you say?" Nolin yells, crouching in front, his right arm quivering. "Has she changed? Tell me, you fuckin' dickhead, or I'll blow your brains all over the wall! Tell me now!"

Peter coughs against the barrel, and Nolin eases back enough for him to get a breath. "I don't know if she's changed. I only just met her. I don't know."

"That's right. You met her, business as usual, was it? First you screw up my life, then you go and screw my girlfriend."

Peter begins to shake his head, then thinks better of it. There's no telling what's going to set Nolin off, and too obvious a lie might do it. Peter is conscious of his own bare feet, as Marina's were when she ran out the door. His feet are throbbing, maybe fractured. But she's safe. Marina is safe. At least there's that.

"Your rust-bucket Bronco parked out front plain as day. But, hey, she's not too fussy these days, that little whore. She's probably fucked half the guys in town."

"No." Peter shifts his eyes carefully from Nolin's own wavering gaze to the hand around the action of the shotgun,

f the main living-room window, which reflects
lights outside.

y to break it to you, man. I really am. She's a little
whore come out of her shell. Just this spring, seems like. But
who knows, huh? Who knows what tricks that slut's been up
to all —"

The telephone rings. Nolin whirls and swings the gun
with him, pointing it crazily at the phone.

Peter takes a deep breath, tries to mentally force back the
pain under his ribs, the throbbing of his skull and swollen
face. When his tongue moves, he feels the sharp stubs of
broken teeth.

The phone rings four times until the voice mail kicks in.
A few moments later it begins to ring again, four times, and
then Nolin picks up the portable phone. "Hello, this is the Faro
residence. Ms. Faro's not in right now. Can I take a message?"
He smiles at himself while listening to the speaker at the other
end. "Hi, Sergeant, yeah, that's right. I played hockey. Don't tell
me, I guess you want my autograph. That's why you're calling?
No shit! Is that you out there in that black rig? I wondered what
all the fuss was about. Yes, sir, I guess I am in breach of my bail
conditions, because I'm fuckin' tired of them. Yeah … nope."

Nolin has the phone and gun in hand now, crawls back
to the narrow window at the foot of the stairs, and slowly lifts
his head to perhaps get a glimpse of whoever he's talking to.
For a moment Peter thinks it's strategy to draw a target for the
snipers in place by now. But no shot comes.

"Oh, he's hangin' in there," Nolin says into the phone.
"Hey, Mr. Bail Supervisor, the sergeant wants to know how
you're doing? Fine, right? Yeah, sorry, Officer, he's tied up at
the moment, but he says he's fine." Nolin laughs. "No … no, I'm
taking it serious enough, I think. Here, let me show you …"

Nolin tosses the phone onto the couch. He scans the room, lifts the stubby shotgun to his shoulder, points it at the window behind the kitchen table, and pulls the trigger. The hammer snaps on the last used shell, so he jacks the pump and pulls again, blasting glass and shreds of white curtain out over the sidewalk and lawn. Peter jumps at the noise, and again he feels the chair shift slightly. His eardrums ring, and the gust of spent powder hits his nose like pepper. Four shells left in the bear buster? He hasn't noticed any more ammunition.

Peter's captor stares at the jagged remains of the window frame and grins as he picks up the phone. "How's that? Serious enough for you? Nope, I don't wanna talk anymore, Chief. You're just pissing me off." Nolin hits the off button on the cordless phone, then stares at it for a moment. By habit, he puts it back almost gently in its grey cradle. "Fuckin' cops, they get to me, man. Don't they get to you, huh? Oh, I forgot. You're kinda like a cop yourself. If I remember right, you have the power to arrest. But right now, shit, you aren't in very good shape to arrest anybody, are you? I said, *are you*?"

"No, I'm not." Peter shakes his head minutely, jostling the vessel of pain. *Nothing good can come of this,* a voice inside him says. *This is lose-lose-lose. Just a question of how much and when. Now wake up. Wake up or it's over.*

"Marina's not a whore," Peter says, no clear thought to where he's going with this.

"What?" Nolin laughs, the shotgun wobbling in his hands, but the muzzle never far removed from Peter's torso. "What did you say?"

"She's not a whore."

Nolin's face jitters in transition from that of unbelief back to hatred. "I should blow your head off right now, you stupid dick. What do you call a bitch who fucks two guys at a house party — oh, I mean, two guys at once? How would you handle that, man? Come home and say, 'Let's have some iced tea and talk, baby, 'cause somebody's spreading nasty rumours about you. People are laughing behind my back!'"

"I don't know."

"What?"

"I don't know how I'd handle that. But life is ... challenging. Everybody has to deal with something. Crosses to bear and all that. I don't know what it's been like for you. But we have choices to make." What other clichés can he apply, what can he babble to keep the dialogue going? "Every day we get a chance to turn things around."

Nolin laughs hard at that. "Oh, yeah, you're getting all warmed up. You should be a TV preacher. You're wasting your time in the probation office."

"Marina wasn't happy. That's not your fault, just the way it is," Peter says, risking a half-truth versus outright deception when either one might trigger his death. "Maybe you knew that, maybe not. How much coke have you done today?"

"Not enough, man, not enough," Nolin snaps. He's sitting in the passageway between the kitchen and the front room, his back to the wall, the shotgun cradled over one knee. He leans there with brute charisma, and the strong-jawed face of a fallen hero. For a moment he seems deathly tired, wiping a film of sweat from his forehead, almost vulnerable. Then chemical want kicks in. He smiles, puts down the shotgun for the first time, and crawls to where his nylon jacket is draped over a kitchen chair. "Not enough. That's more good thinking, man. Fuck, you're smart."

From his jacket pocket he draws a slim black case, and from this a blue glass pipe, along with a nugget in tinfoil and a chrome lighter. It's the neat kit of a serious addict. Peter didn't foresee this, and the situation's lurch makes him nauseous again. Nolin peels apart the foil, gently crumbles some of the rock into the pipe, immediately puts the lighter to the bowl, and inhales. Then again.

Light strobes steadily through the room, along with faint bursts of noise from outside, once a voice with a blowhorn warning neighbours away. The air inside the apartment is polluted by sweat and blood, gunpowder and crack smoke. Several minutes pass. Nolin shudders a bit with pleasure, then paws the floor beside him until his hand finds the shotgun.

This man wants to kill him, Peter knows. Here he sits wrapped like freight to an easy chair, knowing death is now probable. Being straight in the presence of someone very high, you quickly drift apart — and Peter doesn't want that to happen, to be a more obvious target of enemy rage. Nolin fires his lighter, takes another hit off the glass pipe, exhales with a low groan, and then paws for the gun again, his fingers fidgeting with the trigger guard.

"Can I have some of that?"

"What?"

Peter nods toward the pipe. Nolin bursts into laughter, his big white teeth bared, his free hand lifting in a gesture of amazement. "Sure, dude, what the fuck. One last puff, firing-squad style, eh?"

"Something like that."

Nolin crawls forward with the slim black case, places the black gun at Peter's feet, but well out of reach, then rises upright on his knees and extends his hands, offering the blue glass pipe to Peter's lips.

He hasn't tasted cocaine for ten or twelve years. Only a few times altogether, and each time he told himself never again, using logic based on simple facts: one, that any kind of habit will drive a person to bankruptcy; two, that the stuff offers too much pleasure, money be damned, leaving what in its wake? But this hit is free, he's already missed two mortgage payments, and he's taped to a chair facing execution. *What the hell?*

Nolin flicks the lighter over the bowl, and Peter inhales. On previous occasions when he snorted coke he felt the bitter icy sugar film of it in his throat, then the fairly swift high. But crack. This immediate blast like cayenne and honey fills his sinuses and chest, heating his arteries, arms and legs, hands, feet, fingers, and toes. All constricted by packing tape, so that a wave of physical panic goes through him, and this jolt shifts the chair another couple of inches. His tongue plays over jagged stumps of broken teeth, and he tastes his own blood. Every thought brings a tracer-like pain, now diminished somewhat by the drug, but loading his body like a coil spring. His own history, the chronology of personal events over the past year, his job as an officer of the court, the circumstances and his suspect actions that led to this moment, all this washes over him in a prolonged moment of terror and then streams away like trash into black space.

The sense of helplessness diffuses with the rise of anger, last-ditch thinking. As misguided as it might be, Peter is attached to his own life. *So focus, centre yourself.* He thinks of the ocean, the West Coast surf rolling in onto a misty beach. During his last two years of university, he hooked up with a fanatic surfer girl, with the funky Dodge wagon and all, who outfitted Peter with a bodysuit and a board and chased him into the ocean. And there were moments out there, within the mammoth breadth of the water, when he felt at peace with the planet. Better to have loved and lost than never to have loved at all, à la Annie Lennox.

He thinks of skiing with Karen, some of the remote slopes they shared. In his backpack a folding shovel, emergency supplies, and lunch. Sharing cheese and a wineskin, Karen catching the red stream of Chianti in her mouth. Never imagining they would part. Bittersweet life. Marina had in no way displaced Karen in his memory or heart. The relationships were as different as the women themselves. Karen's been gone almost nine months, and Marina about an hour, perhaps more. Peter isn't certain how long he was unconscious, but he's very much awake now, and both women are gone. They're safe, he hopes. But he isn't.

Nolin is prowling from window to window in a crouch, with a good grip on the shotgun. All the dramatized movie and television violence Peter has ingested like anyone else for more than thirty years has in no way prepared him for this, watching a male human with his life on the line, clutching a physical weapon. The black stubby shotgun has its own terrible appeal as a tool of survival. Black as obsidian, like an axe head laced with rawhide onto a curved branch. The human male developed as a hunter, a defender, a warrior; the ethics and conscience came much later and have never fully taken hold at the primal level or altered the species instinct.

"What's the plan?" Peter asks, each short word painful.

"The plan, yeah, yeah, we gotta have a plan!" Nolin laughs a bit too hard at this. Between the rye he's swilled and the crack he's smoked, his senses of humour and perception are now well and truly distorted. But he understands that he's trapped, that his life is at stake, maybe ruined no matter what. His eyes are as wild as those of a snared hyena. "I'm open to suggestions, Officer. You've been so smart so far. You and Miss Smarty-Fucking-Pants Marina make a good pair."

"Okay," Peter says slowly, carefully forming his words, "one plan could be, you call the police. I talk … I can do the talking part. Once they know I'm alive, part of the deal, maybe they'll ease off a bit. Right?"

"Maybe. Then what?"

"Then … you have to throw the gun out the window."

"Fuck that noise!" Nolin scrambles over to wave the gun in Peter's face, then drops the muzzle with a jab against his captive's inner elbow. "How about I blow your arm off and throw it out the window, so they know I'm serious?"

"I'll bleed to death and you'll probably get shot. Seriousness isn't an issue here. They know you're goddamn serious!" Peter's voice rises for the first time, and the strain sends a wave of pain through his mouth and upper body.

"So I'm arrested and go to jail for years. I don't know, man. That plan just don't grab me."

"Maybe not," Peter says, summoning enthusiasm for his lie. "Your lawyer's good, remember? That's what you pay him for. You get a psych assessment, talk about losing Marina, your grief, losing your house, your career. Anybody would be screwed up by all that. I'll be called as a witness. I'll testify about your state of mind. Very depressed, under the influence of alcohol, drugs —"

"You'll testify how you begged me for a hit yourself? Or maybe how you started fucking my girlfriend in the first place on government time?" Nolin nods toward him briefly with a malicious grin, then turns back to the window, even raises his head above the sill to look outside. The drug has made him bolder.

Nolin's last words echo, and for a few seconds Peter slips back toward nausea. The man's mind is impaired, but he has a point. It's not impossible that a good lawyer could portray

Todd Nolin as a victim himself of this chain of events. But for the moment Peter feels he owns the role.

The tape binding his torso has made his lower arms go numb, but fired by the drug, Peter has been flexing his fingers and feels his hands grow warmer with the circulation of his blood. His own blood and sweat smell rank in his nose. Peter shifts his feet flat against the floor, one more painful than the other and maybe broken. He tracks Nolin's every movement with his eyes now. The chair he's taped into is synthetic suede, with low arms, mounted on a round steel frame on the floor. He's felt it move and is hopeful it's not as heavy as it looks. He guesses forty pounds.

Nolin is doing his circuit of the apartment on his feet in a crouch now, his sneakers squeaking on the linoleum, more frantic and careless. He's impatient, far too used to getting his own way, not cut out for an all-night standoff. His voice is vicious. "That goddamn bitch, little nympho freak, dragged me into this!"

"Know something?" Peter says, speaking mainly just to engage him, to be more than the object of hatred. "You're not the only guy who's lost a woman. Happens every day. Happened to me last year. It makes a guy crazy, but nobody's blaming you. Nobody's laughing. We can get out of —"

"Blaming me? No, I don't blame me, neither. I blame that bitch, and I blame you!"

The phone rings.

"Go with the plan, Todd. It's all —"

"Shut up!" Nolin swings the shotgun up in hand, the wavering muzzle less than five feet from Peter's face as he sidesteps to the phone and picks it up on the third ring. "Hello out there." While Nolin listens to the voice at the other end, his eyes are locked on Peter's for most of a minute.

"He's fine, more or less. I hear you. What then is what I'm wondering. That's what I don't hear." Nolin turns his attention from Peter to the living-room window. He positions himself at an angle but steps closer for a better view outside, trying to get a look at the man he's talking to. The shotgun is lowered to his side as his body turns.

Peter plants his feet against the floor fairly wide apart, the sites of his pain competing for attention, all combining to threaten his consciousness. Yet the pain is also a reminder of the stakes, the final pressure on the spring. As Nolin turns his back, straight ahead, Peter heaves forward in the chair. The momentum tips him forward into an impossible squat, with the forty-pound chair strapped to his back. He pushes off with his feet, tucking his head as far as possible at the last moment so that the top of the chair strikes Nolin squarely under the shoulder blades.

Altogether maybe five hundred pounds in motion, two ruined men, a chair, and a shotgun crash through the plate glass.

Six feet to the flower bed, Peter's chair carries him a full rotation. The tuck of his chin saves his life as one corner of the backrest hits the brick retaining wall inches from his skull. He comes to rest like an astronaut facing the sky, amid the cacophony of breaking, raining glass, Nolin's enraged voice, and sharp claps of gunfire. Then the ground itself seems to break beneath him, and Peter begins free fall into a black hole.

chapter twenty-two

Fluorescent light has always been an anathema to Peter, a curse on his nerves, and he awakens flat on his back restrained to the bed, his head immobile in a plastic sling, facing those tubes inset behind the translucent panel in the ceiling. Consciousness brings pain. Tubes are also running into his arm, one from a plastic bag suspended from a chrome stand. The right side of his face feels as if it's pressed against a waffle iron on full heat, his skin seared to a crust. Every breath brings a stab under his ribs. Peter wiggles his fingers easily, but when he tries to move his toes, the left foot seizes and throbs. His tongue grates against the stumps of broken teeth. From the base of his skull to his lower back a deep, dull pain wraps his spine. The only thought that soothes his terror is that if he were paralyzed maybe he wouldn't feel this pain. He can move his limbs, but not his head. He's stuck there facing the lights, and after a minute he closes his eyes again to escape back into the numb haze he's been in for unknown days.

Sometime later he hears a repeated squeak, the soles of the night nurse, and senses her entry into the unit. He keeps his eyes closed while she checks the equipment surrounding him, the red digital readings and fluid lines. She's softly humming a tune that's familiar from the radio, though he can't name the singer or the song. Country. He finds her muted voice a sudden and essential comfort and feels a new ache in his throat. When she turns away, he half opens his eyes to watch her quietly leaving, and the artificial light is blurred by his tears.

After riding out the coma, and semi-coma, the doctors can't say how long Peter will be in the hospital. He's wheeled from the ICU to a shared room on the third floor, the other occupant being a Mr. Raphael, an aboriginal estimated to be something over one hundred years old. A very quiet and dignified roommate, not much for conversation. His old eyes are sometimes open, but he shows no response at all to the nurses, or to the queries Peter has voiced to him when they're left alone. The hospital sits on a hill, so the room offers a good view of the town and the hills to the west. Peter has negotiated with the staff about the fluorescents in the room. Raphael didn't seem to object, and so they're left largely to natural light, and the sunsets each late-summer evening.

Peter is a smorgasbord of injuries: some bones of his left foot are broken, as a result of the chopping gun barrel; two ribs also, one that perforated his lung; the rain of shattered glass cut him in several places, noticeably in a gash along his right jaw, which needed sixteen stitches; two teeth are gone from the other side of his mouth; most seriously overall, one of his neck vertebrae was fractured, which is the reason for the neck brace and sling that immobilizes his head.

"Do you have a mirror?" he asks the nurse one morning. "Can I see?"

"Ah …" she says, studying him sympathetically. "Why not give it a few days, okay?"

"I see."

They feed him puréed meals, like ham and peas, through a straw. After indeterminate days, staring in one direction for hours at a time, he passes through despair and madness into a part chemical, part mystic calm.

One morning he opens his eyes and is surprised to find Laine Perault sitting by his bedside. She's wearing a new black denim shirt. He watches her for a moment before she realizes he's awake.

"Hey, there," she says, "some people will do anything to get a little time off work."

He smiles stiffly, wincing. "Hi."

Laine gives him a little grin, and then her eyes soften in a way he hasn't seen her do before. "I brought a card from the office. And I brought you a coffee from Timmie's, but no straw."

"It's worth a try." He takes the cup from her hand. It's too full for him to tip it toward his lips, so Laine pours half of it down the room sink. Peter then manages a sip, with only a dribble on his neck brace. "Mmm, first one in a while."

"They don't give you coffee?"

"They call it coffee, but they must use recycled grounds or something," he says with some effort. He can tell Laine is getting nervous and needs to be going. He's groggy and nodding off again. Squinting at her, he says, "Thanks."

"Ah," she says, waving her hand, resuming her gruff style, "looks like you might be here a while yet, so like Arnold says, I'll be back!"

The next morning there's a knock at the door, and a deep voice says gently, "Alice?"

Peter opens his eyes, and there's Woodgate towering to one side. The bed is positioned with him looking out the window. So Woodgate brings a chair with him in his giant right hand and cradles his big frame in it so that they're face to face. Peter hasn't yet had a look in the mirror, after the nurse's warning, but he can see himself in the flinch of the man's eyes.

"How … I mean, of course, under the circumstances, how are you doing, Alice?"

Woodgate's appearance and the fact that he mispronounces Ellis with innocent sincerity, nearly makes Peter laugh, but the pain in his side cuts it short. "Okay."

"Well, good …" Woodgate scratches his football skull. "It's a hell of a thing to happen. Can't say as I've been involved with anything quite like this before. And I am involved, as the manager responsible. I've had a few questions to deal with."

"Nolin?"

"Dead. They shot him, because he had hold of the shotgun when he came off the ground. So there's an investigation under way there, but the sergeant isn't too worried. Says it was clean from their end. They interviewed Ms. Faro. And you can expect they'll interview you one day soon."

Crystal ice passes through the arteries of Peter's battered body, a tingling little wave.

Woodgate's eyes lock on Peter's own for a moment. The manager clears his throat in a drawn-out manner. "She said she called you late on the Thursday afternoon. Tammy remembers it was before the office closed, but you didn't take a Jeep."

Peter understands from Woodgate's look that his own response is now of utmost importance. "Well, signing the vehicle in and out … it was the end of the day. I thought on my way home —"

"Right, a shortcut. You didn't ask about overtime. Maybe I wasn't available to sign it off. You didn't anticipate any need to come back to the office. That explains why you took your own vehicle, picked Ms. Faro up, and were planning to help her move a few things to the women's safe house?"

"Right."

Woodgate scratches, like an old primate in a brown suit, and looks away from Peter, out the window. "So it was about four-thirty, maybe four-forty-five, when you arrived at her apartment. If she were going to grab a few things, maybe change her clothes, you would've expected to leave there by five o'clock, have her at the safe house by 5:15. Yet Nolin arrived at approximately 6:30. The landlady called the police at 6:42. And it's that hour and fifteen minutes that's in question. Or that will be in question when I sit down with the director of corrections tomorrow afternoon. He's flying in."

Peter finds himself fascinated by the tone of Woodgate's voice, especially considering the subject matter, subdued, almost gentle. Yes, it's a potential shit storm, headline material. He takes a deep, painful breath. But it's his doing, and he won't drag his sad old manager into it, for God's sake. If he gets out of it without criminal charges himself, obstruction of justice or manslaughter, then he can move on, maybe to the Arctic.

"Ms. Faro explained that she was very distressed. She mentioned dropping the suitcase, which brought you upstairs. After that you began talking. She needed someone to talk to.

She was very distressed. She sat on the bed — it was unmade from the morning. You sat in the green armchair. She got carried away, gave some of her life story. It's not that unusual for people to open up like that under times of stress. Before you knew it, you'd talked for an hour or more."

When Woodgate glances at him, Peter slowly says, "That's right."

"For example, she told you about the death of a boyfriend in high school?"

"Yes … he fell off a cliff, the cliff out at The Ashtray."

"Like that other fellow recently, Nolin's acquaintance, apparently. And it turns out he was involved briefly with Ms. Faro, and now they're thinking maybe Nolin killed him for it."

Peter can't nod or shake his head, or summon much expression to his face. He can talk if need be, or be silent, and for now that's his option. Woodgate has laid it out very well, like a gift.

"Ms. Faro says that's how it happened. You were sitting upstairs, absorbed in your conversation, when Nolin kicked in the door." Woodgate slowly wipes his big hand over his long face. He's in an uncertain amount of pain himself, but he's doing his best to *manage* the situation. "It shows inexperience and poor judgment. And by coincidence, we assume, you were there when Nolin arrived. But it also appears you saved Ms. Faro's life by going well beyond the call of duty, so to speak. That's the position I'm taking on this, the one I'll put to the director."

Peter lies semi-prone, his immobile point of view out the dust-specked window overlooking the city. It takes some effort to shift his gaze even far enough to meet that of Woodgate, and a relief looking back out the window again. Everything depends on perspective. To voice his own, to attempt any reframing, doesn't seem wise.

"Okay … I appreciate that."

Woodgate holds up his hand, doesn't want to hear any more. "By the way, the union actually came through for you. They made the case that you've been on full-time for a year and a half and are overdue for training. So, once you're back in shape, and if you're still interested in being a PO, there's a job for you. There's a permanent position open now, with Robinson moving on. No hurry, though. You've got some mending to do."

The manager rises to his feet, his big frame turned toward the window. He lingers there for a moment in silence, taking in the view. "You know, Alice, I'm six months away from retirement. I'm taking a buyout package next spring. The wife's already booked us on a cruise. I'm sure I strike you as old school, but I'm proud of my career. This situation has the potential for pretty bad press, and I don't need that any more than you do. Less, in fact, because I've got a lot more to lose. I'll recommend you for a Service Award for commitment to public safety, all that. It'll help close the door on questionable circumstances."

"I understand, thank you."

"I have just one piece of advice as your retiring manager," Woodgate says, pausing on his way out the door, an odd glint in his eye. "I spoke with a corporal who was at the scene, and one of the ambulance attendants, about a couple of details. And in future, as a probation officer, during the course of a workday, I advise you to keep your shoes and socks on."

The following morning Peter speaks with his mother by telephone, playing down his injuries, repeatedly assuring her there's no need to get on a plane. She suggests he ask the nurses for extra fruit and that he watch her choice of soap opera at two in the afternoon.

He has this in mind for some amusement, but then has another visitor about that time. Maggie McConachie bustles in, in her navy blue suit, with a blue glass vase of tulips. She's all goodwill embodied in a five-foot full-figured woman. After placing the flowers on the side table, she drags the chair into position and sits down, lays her hands on the edge of his bed, and releases a heartfelt sigh. For a moment her eyes shine with compassion. Her hair is glossy and streaked, artfully framing her face. There is slight rouge on her cheeks and rose lipstick. Lying immobile in bed for a week has a way of focusing one's senses, and Peter catches a teasing hint of her perfume.

"Oh, my," she says, her sharp hazel eyes taking in his bandaged feet protruding from the bottom of the bed, the wrapping around his torso beneath his pajama top, the plastic neck brace and sling apparatus, his face swollen with stitches, the black gap in his teeth. "That must have been a rough day."

"I've had better." He smiles carefully. "Should have taken your advice."

"I won't say I told you so," she quips, then becomes more serious. "But Marina says you saved her life. She's very, very grateful, of course."

"She's okay?"

Maggie hesitates for a moment. "She'll be okay, I think, in time. The things that poor girl's been through."

"If you're talking to her, please say, pass on …"

Maggie looks at him, and her eyes are indecipherable because he wants one thing and won't accept her gentle warning. "If I can, yes, I will, Peter."

She then changes the subject a bit too deliberately. She says the incident made the papers and that she was interviewed for the television news. Peter wonders about Marina, where she is and what she's feeling, and doesn't hear all that Maggie is telling him. After a while, when she rises to leave, she catches his attention, saying the detectives plan to see him the following morning.

He's offered puréed chicken à la king for supper that evening and declines. Likewise for the milky cream of wheat the next morning despite the nurse's admonishment. He settles for lukewarm coffee through a straw and awaits the police with knotted stomach.

Around nine-thirty Detective Spurrier comes in, followed by none other than newly promoted Kevin Bergstrom in training. The former constable is feeling natty in his leather jacket, working out of uniform now. "I run into you in the strangest places," he says. "I always thought probation was a desk job, but you seem to take a different approach."

"The desk will suit me fine for a while after this," Peter says.

"I should say so." Spurrier straddles a chair and meets Peter's eyes with a humourless, inquisitive stare.

Bergstrom remains standing, checking out the room, the old Native in the other bed who's sitting upright with his eyes closed. With his hands in his leather pockets, Bergstrom turns to the window and says, "Nice view, at least, if you've got to lie in bed for a week or two."

Oh, Christ, help me, Peter thinks. *This is going to be a full-on interrogation with all the tricks and second-guessing. I should just come clean. Are you crazy?*

The questions come more or less in chronological order, and Peter lays it out just as Woodgate gave it to him. They've interviewed Marina, and he has only an outline of her version of events. He has no idea, for example, whether they're actually aware of the personal relationship he's had with Marina, but he assumes no, otherwise the jig would be up already. They'd get him for something. Maybe he'd end up on probation himself. This thought actually makes him smile for a moment just when Spurrier asks about Nolin's dive out the window.

The detective notes this expression and frowns. "Something funny?"

"Ah, no, not at all," Peter says, suddenly sombre as can be. "Have you ever been in a car accident?"

"What?" Bergstrom chimes in, questioning Peter's question.

"Well, I was in an accident once, and it was something like that. It takes a few seconds, near death, when things can go either way. And afterward it's hard to piece it all together, makes you wonder, and you have to laugh. Nothing funny about it, though, nothing at all."

Spurrier listens, maybe thinking this is suspect evasive bullshit. However, for whatever reason, as near as they are to a weeping confession, the detective doesn't close in for the kill. He offers only a curt nod. "All right, that should do us." He stands and swings his chair back to exactly where it was.

"Ah, well, I've got one more question," says Bergstrom, the fiery light of a budding detective in his eye. "Your personal vehicle, an '89 Ford Bronco, was at the scene. At, what was it, 6:45, something like that. Is that common practice over at probation, using your own vehicle?"

Peter views Bergstrom at a painful angle, and once again considers saying, *No, your hunch is right. In fact, I was over there in bed with Ms. Faro and we lost track of time. That's the truth, the basis of justice. Isn't that what we're all after?*

"I've covered that point with his supervisor," Spurrier answers, steering his bulk out the doorway. "We've got that."

Bergstrom matches Peter's stare for another moment, then nods on his way out. "I see, okay, we've got that covered."

For the first time in recent memory Peter craves a drink, two fingers of good Scotch over ice. Something to take his brain for a hike in the heather. But it seems he came through the police interview okay. There's no guarantee they won't be back on a new tack. But apparently higher powers are handling this, and no doubt for their own reasons are saving him from sacrifice.

During the course of his stay in hospital, Peter receives cards and calls from family and friends, colleagues, and from other acquaintances, more than he would have anticipated, if he ever imagined himself tied in a metal bed for three weeks.

One of the cards is from Karen, which surprises him most of all. Enclosed is a two-page letter. She heard via an unnamed friend that he was in the hospital, wishing him the best, and so on. Also, the real-estate agent called her and might have a buyer for the house. She was prepared to accept any reasonable offer. Danica, her partner, exhibited her work in San Francisco and apparently made quite a splash. They want to expand her studio, looked forward to doing the work themselves.

Peter has no trouble imagining Karen organizing such a project. Whereas he wouldn't trust himself to mix a bag of cement, she'll be out there with a transit, skill saw, nail gun. Knocking off come sunset in California, and here comes Danica in her paint-splattered T-shirt, bearing Coronas and lime. For the first time in thirteen days, Peter feels a sexual stirring, which comes with great and almost humorous relief. As well, he's deeply touched by Karen's concern and the letter. His hope for her friendship rises from the dead.

One day the nurse brings him a paper bag taped shut, saying a woman dropped it off for him at reception. Inside he finds three paperback novels by John le Carré, Elmore Leonard, and an author unknown to him. There's also a postcard from a Rocky Mountain park, a photo of a waterfall, and on the flip side a note wishing him well from Sarah Moxey. Perhaps Karen got the news from her. The books are a godsend, and he thinks about Sarah a bit between chapters. Perhaps she and Karen are in touch. He doesn't understand her apparent interest in him, partly because she's quite attractive, in an earthy way, and surely not at a loss for companionship. But he must thank her for the books, especially intuiting his taste.

A few other people from the probation office pop in for brief visits. It seems they might be taking turns, and he appreciates that also. After Karen left, Peter felt increasingly isolated, with few friends he could call his own. It's reassuring that people know he's alive. After two weeks, he loses count of the days and finds a curious security lying there day after day, absolutely sober apart from the clear, diminishing painkiller fed into him via a coiled tube and needle taped to his arm. Plenty of time to think.

The centurion Mr. Raphael provides silent companionship throughout. Every morning the nurse elevates his bed, the old man takes his coffee black with three packets of sugar prepared by the nurse, and a few strips of bacon. Now there's a diet to live on for a hundred years. A few times a day, with no one else around, Peter says something aloud. He no longer speaks directly to Raphael, because there's never been any form of reply, just voices thoughts, to test reality or break the silence.

For almost three weeks the old man follows the same Spartan daily routine, eyes open once in a while, taking in the weather, perhaps as he first did as a child by the river as his mother cleaned salmon and hung them on pine pole racks to dry. While Peter has had more visitors than he expected, the old man hasn't had one until today. It's mid-afternoon, and Peter is dozing himself when he hears someone speak in a very different tongue. Then there's a hoarse reply from Raphael. Peter's eyes and ears open, suddenly alert, and though he can't see the person, nor understand the words of Secwepemc, the visitor's voice is oddly familiar. The old man's replies are slow and sparse, eerily different from English, yet somehow calming.

When the tall frame of the visitor's back falls within his view, Peter says, "Levi?"

"Bail man? You look like you been dragged behind a horse."

"I pretty much feel it, too, but not as bad as I did a week ago. What brings you here?"

"This man," he says, gesturing at the old fellow, "my mother was his spirit sister."

"He's your uncle?"

"Close enough … for English." Then he speaks Secwepemc to Raphael, who nods and slowly responds, but doesn't shift his gaze. "Pleased to meet you, he says. He says you talk sometimes, but he doesn't know English."

"Pleased to meet him also. Yes, it's a bad habit I have, talking to myself."

The old man volunteers another whispered comment. Levi nods. "He says he sees a woman in your heart. Maybe you speak to her?"

"What?" Peter asks, incredulous.

"Some elders live a long time, some live to see what's comin', or speak with ancestors. Some, like Raphael, can see into a person's heart."

"No kidding? That's amazing." He doesn't wish to show skepticism or any disrespect. And, in fact, many of his waking hours have been spent thinking of Marina. Perhaps he's even spoken her name. "Like you said that night at the rodeo grounds, Levi, there's always a woman or two involved."

Levi repeats this for Raphael, and the three of them share a chuckle.

Later on, deep in the sleepless night and the muted gloom of the hospital, after going over every possible reason and speculation, he finally must accept he hasn't heard from Marina. No message, no call, no card.

Her face won't leave his mind, though, the ferocious look in her eyes when she first realized Nolin was in her home that terrible evening. No longer a victim, she found something stronger than fear inside herself.

Initially, he thought or dreamed he could feel her thinking of him, but no longer. They broke rules, and perhaps only used each other in a way as life preservers when both were at risk of drowning. She must know that he does care for her, at least he hangs on to that hope. But she's putting time and plenty of distance between them.

chapter twenty-three

On the morning of his release from the hospital, Peter stands outside on the curb in the sunshine and passing shade of afternoon clouds, awaiting his cab. He wears a neck brace, new clothes, and runners billed to his health care card, with a plastic bag holding his acquired toiletries over the past three weeks, the cards, magazines, and paperbacks. Off to the left is a woman in a wheelchair with a stainless-steel oxygen and medication stand connected to her via tubes and a mask, the mouthpiece pushed to one side so she can enjoy another cigarette. There's a cluster of other worried family members huddled in discussion about someone else lying somewhere in a room upstairs. To his right is the ambulance bay, the grey asphalt parking lane and trolley access sidewalk marked in stark white lines.

His entire body is stiff and aching, his face still swollen along the red seam of stitches along his jaw. During the time he was unconscious, they shaved his hair. Now grown out three weeks, it's a rough, dark thatch with new hints of grey at his temples. A slight breeze carries the dry scents of summer, lawn clippings, and green apples. He's glad to be out. But as if imprisoned for years, his circumstances now feel very unfamiliar. He doesn't know exactly what to do with himself. The cab arrives, and Peter eases himself into the back seat.

From her hideaway in California, via email and telephone, Karen managed the sale of their house. He should be more grateful, rescued from the sea of personal bankruptcy. The price isn't bad. It will clear the mortgage, and after real-estate fees and bank penalties, leave them each with a few thousand dollars. A sad net worth at his age, but better than being in the hole.

The manicured agent brings papers out one morning, lays them out at the kitchen table, clearly uneasy with Peter's POW appearance. She smells like a mango tree. He wears a frayed green rugby shirt, khaki shorts, and bare feet. Then there's the three-inch-thick white plastic neck collar, broken teeth, and the healing purple gash along his left jawbone. He's made coffee, but she declines, wired enough anticipating her percentage on the deal. A last-minute request is occupancy within two weeks. The buyers are new to town, currently living in a motel, eager to take possession. Peter absorbs this information, lights a cigarette, and ponders the matter for a few minutes while sipping his coffee, taking a hit of satisfaction from the agent's discomfort, letting her wonder for a minute or two. He really has no choice. On several pages, at each point flagged by a stick-on pink tab, he sees Karen's assertive signature in the blue felt tip ink she's always favoured, and beside these he scribbles his own in black ballpoint. It's the last time their names will ever appear side by side, and it saddens him. The agent couldn't be happier. She's on her feet and snaps the document from his hands into her sharkskin briefcase.

After she's gone, the stove clock reads 11:22. He reaches into the cupboard over the fridge and brings out a half-full bottle of Stolichnaya and mixes a Greyhound, two fingers in a tall glass with ice and grapefruit juice. He takes the drink outside and sits on the step of the weathered back deck in the bold late-summer sunshine.

The yard is overgrown, fringed by knee-high dandelions and thistles. A responsible seller would fire up the lawn mower. But Peter isn't up to wrestling with the mower, and he rather likes the yard the way it is, for the next ten days or so. The house needs work, the windows cleaned, carpets, hell. Pay somebody later. He's got to pack his belongings, which will take a day or two, and what then? Where? He's got to figure out where he'll move the boxes and furniture to. He's got to find an apartment or a motel room.

It's a few days more before he's limber enough to do much packing or to drive. Once he is, he takes a run through town and drives by Arbour Villa twice, where the curtains in unit 5 are open, the windows have been replaced, and the rooms look empty. He circles the block once more and finally pulls into the lot. Peter spots Fay Kubova at the back corner of the lawn, now eyeballing him. He walks in slow motion, glancing at door 5, stricken with flashbacks from his last visit, the beating, the gunfire. And the hour prior to that, upstairs in bed with Marina.

"She isn't here," Mrs. Kubova informs him before he can open his mouth, waving the watering wand as if she might turn it on him.

"I wondered if she maybe left a forwarding address?" he can't help asking, though he knows it's hopeless.

"No!" the old woman barks. "And if she did, I wouldn't give it to you. I don't care what kind of officer you are."

"I'm here only as a friend."

"A friend?" She shakes her head. "Well, go now please. You're no better than the other one. You have no friend and no business here."

He drives away, home to a house full of boxes.

Peter gives some thought to Woodgate's job offer. If he wants to leave this line of work, the service of justice and public safety, now seems the natural time. He's escaped the past few months of insanity without criminal charges against himself, and his injuries will heal, his teeth will be replaced. He could go back to teaching, or maybe small-town journalism, documenting civic politics and bowling league standings. Or he can load up the Bronco and leave town. Nobody will miss him. Start afresh in Winnipeg or Yellowknife. Thing is, he misses the work already, as strange as that might seem to many people. Working with offenders isn't a glorious profession. In fact, for the most part, it's thankless, but for him it has a solid meaning.

During the first days in the hospital, once he was conscious, no longer dreaming of iguanas, smoking fields, and rivulets of hot lava, as soon as he surfaced, he thought only of Marina. Her dark eyes, her face, her beautiful hair. He imagined her limbs, the deep blue dolphin tattoo on her hip, and her curious webbed toes. Her tender heart, his own heart weighed down by his sad mind. His desire for her has only brought her more grief. She's a young woman, she's had only a few lovers, and three of them have died violent deaths. Peter has played a hand, not entirely unwitting, in her tragedy.

What hand he played in Nolin's death is a less-anguished question, but more complex. Probation officers are trained in the management of risk, to document steps taken, and then, locking up the file drawers before they leave the office at five o'clock, they cross their fingers. One can't personally take on the future offences by clients, because these are inevitable. It's only fodder for nightmares. Every once in a while a file goes "sideways," as they say, and sometimes requires an internal investigation. And on that scale the Nolin file is right off the map. He was a steroid gorilla, with all the wrong appetites of a psychopath. His life was a waste, and he lost the chance to change. That's one thing that troubles Peter deeply and always will. Maybe the only real meaning in life is change, evolution in oneself. Probably if they knew the facts, many of his colleagues, maybe most anyone, would argue that out of sheer decency Peter Ellis should resign, never mind that it seems he's escaped punishment, other than some facial disfigurement and an undetermined sense of guilt for the rest of his life.

He locates a cabin to rent on a property bordering untended range with cattle and horses grazing in sight. The landlord seems easygoing. There's a shed to store his skis and bike. In the dusty process of moving, lifting cardboard boxes into and out of the Bronco, Peter feels his life has been factored out, maybe not to the lowest denominator, but damn near. Less than one year ago he lived a modest dream, and Karen conceiving a child was foremost in their minds. Now he's down to this. And he's reminded of certain clients, offenders, not the run-of-the-mill but middle-class guys with no previous records, who make one bad mistake and it tips them into a nosedive. Everyone changes one way or the other.

In the drugstore, Peter buys a package of stationery and envelopes, and sitting on the porch of his cabin, writes a series of thank-you notes to those who sent cards and flowers to the hospital. He labours longest over the note to Karen, discards his first draft, then fixes himself a drink. Peter makes the second as simple as he can bear. He'll always love her, yet senses they might drift away into very different lives and one day lose touch. He doesn't want that, can't face the thought right now, and tries to avoid a gloomy tone while putting this into words.

The cabin has no yard to speak of but is surrounded by brush and range grass, junipers, and a few craggy old pines. The place is barely insulated and heats up something fierce during the day. He spends the evening hours out on the porch, sipping cold beer. The cat flakes out under the wooden steps.

When he's sent off his thanks to everyone else, Peter realizes he has no address for Sarah Moxey, but she jotted her phone number on the card she left with the books. He did appreciate the loan of them. All his other principles may be in serious question, but he is still compelled to return books to their rightful owner. So one evening he calls her.

"Ah, Peter Ellis calling. I wanted to thank you for the books and note …"

"Oh, you're welcome. I thought you'd need some reading material. You survived the hospital? Are you back at work?"

"Yes … no," he says.

"What?"

"I mean, I'm out of the hospital but will be off work for a while, I guess. I wanted to return the books but didn't have your address."

"Well, that's easy." She laughs, recites her address, and adds, "Why don't you come by for dinner tomorrow night and bring them with you?"

Offhand he can think of no excuse, and it will seem rude to invent one, or to turn her down again. "All right, thank you, I will."

"What are some of your favourite foods?"

"Oh, I'm keen on anything, even goat kidneys, oysters, stuff like that. Mediterranean, Indian, Thai, you name it."

"Cajun?"

He arrives about seven the next evening as requested. A young girl in pajamas answers the door, turns, and shouts for her mom. From out of the kitchen Sarah appears with a big smile, her red hair in a loose, unruly braid.

"Welcome, Peter," she says, slipping one hand over the girl's shoulder. "This is Jessica."

"Hi," says the girl, looking up at him wide-eyed. "Are you a priest?"

They laugh about it later, once Jessie is tucked into bed. Sarah passes him the corkscrew, and Peter opens the Shiraz he brought along. The aroma from the kitchen makes his stomach growl. He paces slowly into the dining area and back to the kitchen as Sarah speaks.

"She's rarely seen a priest, I must say. But that collar does give you a clerical look of sorts."

"The priest from hell?" He gingerly touches the red seam left by the stitches along his jaw.

"Something like that!" She laughs, her blue eyes flashing. Her face is well accented with freckles, without makeup. She stirs what he's hoping is gumbo and takes a final taste from her wooden spoon. As they chat, her pace puts him at ease, and there seems no discomfort with silence, either.

"I couldn't find any goat kidneys, but we have some

oysters to start," she says, laying out the first dish.

"Wow!" he says, wiping his mouth after the second bite. "These are fantastic. Is that cornmeal?"

"Yes, it makes them brown nicely in the olive oil. They're topped with shallots, basil, and Romano and finished under the grill."

This is followed by the anticipated gumbo, with prawns and chorizo, along with fresh okra. He can't remember when he last enjoyed food as much as this. At one point, with his mouth full, he meets Sarah's quizzical gaze, and he's momentarily embarrassed by his own appetite. She seems pleased.

"This is a very nice wine," she says, sipping from her glass with poise.

Peter shelled out twenty-four dollars for the bottle and is now glad, because anything less wouldn't have done justice to Sarah's meal. He shrugs. "I saw Mendocino on the label. I've always liked the sound of that."

"Talk to me of Mendocino." She smiles, he gives a sheepish nod, and she hums the tune by Kate McGarrigle as she clears the table.

While in the vicinity of California, he mentions the card from Karen, the sale of the house. "Sounds like she's doing okay down there."

Sarah returns to her chair and pours them each more of the wine. "It must have been very difficult, Peter, after she left."

For a few moments he can't find his voice and leans his braced neck to one side, avoiding her eyes. Finally, he replies, "Yes, it was."

"I understand if you don't want to talk about it," she says quietly, leaning toward him, forearms resting on the wooden table. "But I'll listen if you do."

They sit in silence again. Peter isn't certain what to say, but Sarah's manner and calm blue eyes are reassuring. The house is quiet, and she's opened the dining-room French doors to let in the fragrant evening air. He takes a drink of wine, and a breath, and begins the story.

More Great Castle Street Mysteries from Dundurn

Still Waters
A Quin and Morgan Mystery
by John Moss
978-1-55002-813-3 / $11.99

For Toronto police detectives David Morgan and Miranda Quin, what begins as a routine murder investigation following the discovery of a millionaire's body in his Rosedale koi pond quickly spirals into a series of unspeakable revelations, culminating with Miranda's horrific confinement in the serial killer's slaughterhouse.

Depth of Field
A Granville Island Mystery
by Michael Blair
978-1-55002-855-3 / $11.99

When photographer Tom McCall's partner, Bobbi, is brutally beaten and left for 'dead en route to an assignment photographing the beautiful Anna Waverley's boat for a potential buyer, it's up to Tom to search for an explanation for the attack. But not all is what it seems, among them Anna Waverley.

Also by Christian Petersen

Let the Day Perish
978-0-88878-400-1 / $16.95

In this collection of short stories, Christian Petersen beautifully reins in the confusion and displacement of a diminishing band of men facing the daily spectre of an unforgiving land, men enslaved to the grind of the sawmill, hunkered on bar stools, or wild behind the wheel speeding down dirt roads to the Fraser River in British Columbia.

Tell us your story! What did you think of this book? Join the conversation at www.definingcanada.ca/tell-your-story by telling us what you think.

Available at your
favourite bookseller.

DUNDURN PRESS
www.dundurn.com